THE BLACK
RECRUIT

Cover design by Wendy Bentley

CHAPTER ONE

Maleek and his brother carefully removed all of the safety lights on the garbage truck to prepare for blasting the paint and rust so the company could re-paint it. This was a business the two had started just after Maleek was given a medical disability separation from the Police Department.

The next stage was placing a tarp over the cab to protect the windows from the air blown coal slag that would strip the body of the truck bare. Maleek would don headgear to protect him from the spray and perform the actual blasting while his brother would heft the one hundred pound bags of slag and make sure the air compressor functioned properly as it would provide oxygen to Maleek for the six hour process.

The detail work required to remove the paint and rust was the best part of Maleek's day as it required his total concentration, and did not allow for him to see the young boy's eyes staring into the deepest part of his soul asking, "Mister, why did you have to kill me?."

***

Mattie Williams was born into the poverty of Southern Mississippi to an unwed mother. She would never know who her father was and she was raised in a one room shack which was at the end of a dirt road. The shack had no electricity, running water or plumbing. There was an old bathtub in the yard which was used for washing clothes and bathing. A garden outside provided the primary food source for both Mattie and her mother and a wood burning pot belly stove provided the hot water to wash and bathe as well as the cooking method for the vegetables.

Shortly after her birth, Mattie's mother would leave her alone on a fenced-in mattress while she went to work cleaning houses for the rich people on the other side of town. Her mother would change her diaper and breast feed her before placing her into the bed. Mattie would scream and cry until she would fall asleep. When her mother returned, she would change her diaper and breast feed her again. The dirty diapers would be placed into a drum and then burned with the other trash that was generated.

As Mattie got older she stopped crying and that would define her as a person. When it was time to start school, her mother would walk her to the school before taking the bus to the house that she would clean that day. Because of her financial status Mattie qualified for free breakfast, lunch and an after school snack every day. She would remain at the school until her mother would arrive walk her home every day.

That ended when Mattie started the third grade. After that Mattie would walk alone in the darkness of the morning to and from school. She showed no fear of walking alone in the darkness, where fear would overwhelm most children of that age.

Mattie would stay after school to complete her homework so that she did not have to carry books the three blocks that she had to walk. As she grew older she would bring home one book from the library to read until it got dark and on weekends and she tended to the outdoor garden which had potatoes, beets, greens that would be their primary food source. Her mother would bring home leftover chicken, fish and beef from the homes that she cleaned.. She became more and more determined that she would not have to live a life in a shack when she grew up.

She liked reading books about children who enjoyed their lives and had fun. She dreamed of visiting far-away places like London, Paris, Berlin and Canada. When it came time to graduate, Mattie attended the ceremony alone and went to the celebration to see proud parents hugging their children. The teachers and staff of the school made it a point to come over and hug and congratulate Mattie on the accomplishment. It was a sad and lonely walk home that night, because Mattie had no idea what love was and how it was shown to children.

CHAPTER TWO

The high school was just over a mile from Mattie's shack. Because the school had a two mile minimum radius for bus service, Mattie had to walk to and from the school. From the first day, she felt tension and jealousy in the hallways of the school. Mattie had developed the body of a twenty year old woman as a fourteen year old child. She had a breast size of 38c, a 24 inch waist, and a 36 inch hips. The boys could not take their eyes off of her, while the girls snubbed her. She would sit at the lunch table and no one would even talk to her. The one positive that she had was that her mother was able to get her hand-me-downs from the rich kids, so she was able to impress with her clothing.

Mattie again stayed at school to do all of her homework and worked hard to keep her grades up. Her mother would mark her report cards with an "X" because she had never learned how to read or write. When football season arrived Mattie would stay at school to attend all of the games. On away games she would ride the bus and one of the teachers or staff would buy her ticket to watch the games. Mattie fantasized about becoming a varsity cheerleader when she reach her Junior year. She was sad when football season ended.

Mattie left school and was walking home when a car pulled up next to her and stopped. The passenger window rolled down and Mattie bent down to look inside the new car. She saw the blonde quarterback of the football team driving the car and he said, "Hop in, I will give you a ride home." Mattie got into the car and the quarterback drove her to her road. He looked at her and said, "Be in the same place every day and I will pick you up." He drove her home all that week. On Friday, he asked Mattie, "Would you like to see the secret place where I go to relax? We can pick up dinner and have a picnic." Mattie thought for a second and simply said "Okay." The quarterback drove to a local pizza parlor and picked up a medium pizza for them to share. He drove to the other side of the town and turned down a dirt road. When they reached the end of the road, Mattie saw a grass area surrounded by large trees with a lake at the end of the tree line. The quarterback grabbed a blanket from the car and spread it out on the ground and they ate the pizza and drank lemonade overlooking the crystal clear lake water. When they were done eating, the quarterback picked up all the trash and folded the blanket up to assure the area remained pristine. He drove her back to her road and told her he would see her on Monday at school.

The next week he picked her up every day and dropped her off. When Friday rolled around, he asked her again if she would like to go to the lake. Mattie smiled and said, "Of course I would." This time he picked up hamburgers and French fries for them to eat and set up the blanket on the ground. After they finished their food, he asked Mattie, "Would you like to go swimming with me?" Mattie smiled and replied, "I don't have a bathing suit." The quarterback said, "Neither do I, but no one ever comes back here so I swim naked." Mattie looked confused and said, "I don't know about that. I have never seen a boy naked." The quarterback just laughed and said, "It is nothing but a swim, come on and join me." He removed his shirt and t-shirt and Mattie could see his muscular body. Next he removed his pants and underwear and looked at Mattie to see what she would do. Mattie removed her blouse and bra showing her fully developed breasts and large nipples and then removed her skirt and panties. As she was just forming pubic hair, her vagina was clearly visible and caused the quarterback's manhood to react. He grabbed Mattie's hand and lightly pulled her into the water where they splashed and played in the water. After about 15 minutes, he motioned for her to follow him out of the water and went to the car to grab two bath towels to dry them. They dressed and he drove her home. She was smiling ear to ear from the experience.

The next Friday Mattie ran from the school in anticipation of another evening of fun. The quarterback stopped at a southern cooking restaurant and picked up fried chicken and greens for them to enjoy. After dinner, they again got naked and played in the cool water. After they had both dried off, the quarterback pulled Mattie toward him and kissed her on the lips. Mattie had never been kissed before and liked that part of the experience, but was scared when he pulled her tight to him and she could feel his erection making contact with her body. The quarterback looked into her wide eyes and said, "I think I am falling in love with you Mattie." Mattie was not sure how to react to this. She remembered hearing girls in the school talking about giving their boyfriends a blowjob rather than allowing them to penetrate them. One of the girl's went into detail and Mattie wanted to please this boy because she enjoyed their time together. Mattie dropped down to her knees and lightly grabbed the quarterback's appendage, softly licking on the head before putting it into her mouth. He was softly moaning as she tried to

take it deeper and deeper into her mouth. She heard
him grunt as his juices shot into her mouth causing
her to gag. She did not like the salty taste of his
juices, but did not want to lose the opportunity he
gave her to enjoy life.

The two made the trek to the secluded area every
Friday through the school year. On the days that it
was too chilly or raining, they would eat in the car and
just talk. The week before school was to end for the
year, they made the drive to the lake. It was a
beautiful afternoon with a warm sun, so they went
swimming after they finished the meal. They were
splashing each other and giggling when Mattie turned
away from the quarterback. He grabbed her by her
hips and pulled her toward him until he penetrated
her. Mattie screamed in pain as he pushed inward
and then she heard him grunt and felt the pulsations
of his juices flowing into her. He remained motionless
until the pulsating stopped and then slowly pulled out
of her. Mattie wheeled around with her eyes shooting
flames. The boy started blushing and would not even
make eye contact with her.

He walked back up on land and held a towel out for
Mattie. She wiped herself with the towel, but when
she wiped between her legs, the towel was covered
with blood. She screamed again and threw the towel
to the ground. They both dressed and not a word was
spoken on the way home.

When she returned to school on Monday, there was
no car waiting for her on the street and she walked
home that day and the rest of the days until school
ended.

Mattie signed up for summer programs that offered college credits because she had a burning desire to learn. She did not expect the quarterback to be there and she was correct. When the football program started practicing in early August, Mattie would go to the practices each day. The quarterback did not acknowledge her presence in the stands and there were no more rides home for her.

On the first day of school Mattie was feeling nauseated, but attended anyway. The second day she was in her Civics class when she started feeling really sick. She raised her hand and said, "I am not feeling well and need to see the nurse." Mattie walked into the nurse's office and explained her symptoms to the nurse. The nurse did a check-up and told Mattie that she did not have a fever, but that her blood pressure was elevated. She told Mattie, "I have one more test I need to run. Please take this cup into the bathroom and pee in it for me." When Mattie brought out the full cup, the nurse went to a cabinet and got out an early pregnancy test kit. When the test showed positive, the nurse went back to the cabinet and retrieved a second kit. When it too tested positive, the nurse told Mattie, "Because of your age, I am required by law to submit this sample to the County Department of Health for a definitive test because this test says you are pregnant. The results will be back in a couple of days."

Mattie was in her morning English class when the room door opened and the school secretary announced, "I need Mattie Williams to come with me." Mattie got up and the two walked down the hall without speaking a word. When they arrived at the nurse's office, the secretary simply pointed toward the door and kept on walking.

Mattie saw a man and a woman standing nearby in business suits. She could see gold badges attached to their belts and saw the outline of a gun on the male. Mattie walked into the office and the nurse told her to sit down. The nurse said, "The results came back and you are, in fact, pregnant. Because of your age, state law requires me to call the police and the officers outside want to speak to you." With that the nurse walked out of the room. The two officers entered and the female pulled up a chair next to Mattie. She said, "Hi Mattie, my name is Detective Lori Wheeler and this is my partner Detective Overstreet. We need to ask you who the father of your baby is." Mattie looked at the detective and said softly, "I do not believe that I am required to talk to you. May I please return to my class?" With that Mattie got up and tried to leave the office, but the burly male was standing in the doorway. Mattie looked at the female again and asked, "Am I not free to leave?" The female nodded and her partner moved out of the doorway. At lunchtime Mattie was walking toward the cafeteria and noticed that conversations stopped or reduced to whispers as she approached and that everyone was staring at her. She set her lunch tray down at a table that had two girls already seated, but they immediately picked up their trays and went to another table.

When the day finally ended Mattie almost ran out the door. She was walking toward the street when she saw a car parked on the street that she immediately recognized. When she got close enough she heard a voice say, "Mattie, let me give you a ride home. We need to talk." Mattie got into the car and the quarterback said, "I heard that the cops talked to you this morning, did you tell them it was me?" Mattie looked at the blonde boy and read the fear across his face and said, "I didn't tell them nothing." There was a look of relief of the boy's face. He said, "The University of Florida would withdraw my football scholarship if they knew about this. Thank you for not telling on me. Mattie glared at him and replied, "I didn't do this for you. It ain't none of their business what I do.

The boy thought for a moment and said, "I told my parents what happened and they told me to tell you that they would pay for an abortion if that is what you want." Mattie's eyes showed the same rage as it did at the lake. She looked into the boy's eyes and sternly said, "Ain't no one killing my baby!" The boy reached into the center console and pulled out a cell phone and a business card. He looked at Mattie and said, "My parents thought about that as well. They said they will take care of all of your care throughout your pregnancy. Call the number on the card whenever you are ready and tell them your name. They will set you up." They pulled up to her road and she got out of the car without another word spoken. That would be the last contact the two would have. Whenever Mattie saw him in the halls, he would abruptly change direction and avoid any possible contact.

Mattie called the clinic and gave the woman who answered her name. The woman told her that the doctor needed to see her for a pre-natal examination and that the clinic would send a car to pick her up at school and then return her to school after the visit. They set up a time for the appointment.

Things at the school were deteriorating quickly because Mattie was beginning to show her pregnancy. Mattie would hear the girls whisper names like slut, whore and tramp and the boys treated her like she had a contagious disease. After a couple of weeks of this Mattie had enough. She walked into the office and told the secretary that she wanted to quit school. The secretary looked up her records and told Mattie, "The State of Mississippi does not allow anyone to quit until after their sixteenth birthday," Mattie stormed out of the office and went back to her class.

The clinic set her with training on pregnancy and raising a baby and provided her with material to read. They also measured her body size to get her maternity clothes. The clothing was delivered to her at her home and included elastic pants and blouses for her to wear.

***

Mattie was sitting outside when she started feeling pains which she knew to be contractions. She dialed the clinic and they told her they would send an ambulance to pick her up. Minutes later Mattie heard the sound of a siren and shortly after an ambulance backed into the dirt road. They placed her on a gurney and took her to the clinic.

She was put in a hospital room and examined by a doctor. They did a complete physical examination and determined that she actually was ready to give birth. Several hours later she had a boy and named him Jameel. They kept her in her room for two days to allow her to learn how to breastfeed and change the baby.

When she returned home her mother did not say anything about her pregnancy or the birth. A van pulled up at the shack and a man dropped off boxes containing diapers, baby wipes, baby clothes, formula, a crib with blankets and a stroller for the baby. Mattie had to walk to school carrying the baby and then drop him off with the school's day care, then pick him up.

On her sixteenth birthday Mattie walked to the school and directly into the office. She looked at the secretary and said, "Today is my sixteenth birthday and I officially quit school." After signing a few forms, the secretary told Mattie that she was officially unenrolled from the school.

CHAPTER THREE

Mattie would sit outside the shack during the day and watch her baby grow. Baby food and other necessities continued to be delivered on a weekly basis.

It had now been three months since she had left school and she was outside watching the baby play in his crib. She heard the sound of an engine coming toward her and saw a black Cadillac pull up to the house. A black man got out of the driver's seat and he walked up to Mattie. The young man looked at Mattie and said, "You probably don't remember me, but I know you from school. My name is Tamir and I was wondering if you would like to go get some food." Mattie said, "I don't remember you and I have the baby, so I can't go nowhere." Tamir said,, "Bring the baby with you. Let's go eat, nothing more."

Mattie wrapped Jameel in a blanket and got into the Cadillac. He took her to a southern restaurant on the other side of town and they ate a meal. It was the first real food Mattie had since giving birth. As they were finishing their dinner the waitress walked up to the table and laid down the check. Tamir reached into his pocket and pulled out a large wad of bills. He peeled off a twenty dollar bill and laid it on top of the check. He peeled off a second twenty and handed it to the waitress saying, "This is for you." The waitress smiled and said, "Thank you, it was a pleasure to serve you, Next time you are here, please ask for me. My name is Janice." Tamir was nothing but a gentleman and, when he dropped her back at the shack, he said, "I will stop by soon and we can do this again.

The next time Tamir stopped by he pointed to the rear seat of the Caddy where there was a brand new child safety seat. This time he took Mattie to a restaurant specializing in their barbeque ribs. Mattie loved the spicy taste of the sauce. They talked about Mattie's dreams for the future and her love of reading and learning.

Tamir came and picked Mattie and the baby up and drove them the fifty miles to Montgomery to see the zoo. Mattie had never seen animals other than dogs and cats, so she was wide-eyed when they got to the hippos and gorillas. She especially liked the exotic birds because she had read about them in the books she had read.

Each time Tamir would come, he would introduce Mattie to a new experience. He would come to the house with toys for Jameel and small gifts for Mattie and she was really beginning to like him.

Tamir arrived and told Mattie she needed to dress up for dinner because they were going to a top flight steak house. Mattie found some clothes that her mother had brought home and was sharply dressed for the experience. They arrived at the maître d's counter and the short man asked, "Do you have a reservation?" Tamir reached into his pocket and placed a fifty on the counter replying, "I don't know, do I?" The man picked up the bill and said, "Please follow me." Tamir said, "Mattie, I will order for you this time. You are going to get a steak, baked potato with butter and sour cream and asparagus stems." When the food arrived, Mattie was impressed at the flavor of each of the items he had ordered for her. They were finishing up their dinner when Tamir said, "Mattie, your living arrangements are not conducive to raising a child. Let me find you a place to live where there is air conditioning, a kitchen and a bedroom. We can look tomorrow." Mattie thought for a moment and said, "I like the idea, but how am I supposed to pay for it?" Tamir just laughed and said, "Paying for it is not an issue. I need to find a place to crash during the day as most of my business occurs at night. I am not looking for anything other than maybe some cooking, keeping the place clean and doing some laundry. Take some time to think about it and let me know when I stop over tomorrow."

Tamir pulled into the road and Mattie was sitting in front of the house. She and the baby got into the car and they drove into town. Tamir parked and car and they walked a short distance to a door to a second floor apartment. The apartment had one bedroom, a full kitchen, a large and a small walk-in closet and a large space for a family room and dining area. Tamir asked, "Does this have enough room for you and the baby?" Mattie nodded her head in the affirmative and Tamir looked at the landlord and said, "We will take it."

He took her to a furniture store where she picked out a king size bed, a plush couch, a dining room table, lamps, a sixty inch television, a washer and dryer and a set of drawers to hold clothing. Tamir paid cash for all of the furniture and demanded it be delivered the same day. Next he took her to a Target and bought needed kitchen necessities of plates, silverware and pots and pans, as well as sheets and blankets for the bed. He loaded those items into the Cadillac and then drove Mattie back to the shack, telling her, "Get whatever you need or want because you will not be returning here."

It did not take long for Mattie to get comfortable in this new environment. As Tamir promised, he would sleep in the bed during the day and be out all night. Mattie would sit on the couch and watch the big screen television and play with her son. She liked watching the Food Network to learn new dishes to make for Tamir.

Mattie would wash Tamir's clothes and place them folded on the bed because, for some unknown reason, Tamir had installed a lock on the door to the smaller closet. The large closet was for her.

Tamir had not come to the apartment when Mattie woke up. She heard a commotion coming from outside the door and went to investigate. When she opened the door, she saw Tamir and four burly men struggling to get a cherry wood door up the steps. When they got it to the entrance, Tamir said this would be their new door to keep her safe when he was out doing business. It took the four men two hours to install the door which slid open and closed rather than opened and closed. Tamir handed Mattie a buzzer which unlocked the door and its three separate locks electronically. The door was extremely thick because it had metal rods placed throughout the door.

Mattie would only leave the apartment to buy groceries. She would call a taxicab and she was totally comfortable not having to leave. She was able to focus her total attention on Jameel and was loving every minute of her new life.

Tamir had lived up to his word. If he arrived home before Mattie woke up, she would find him in the bed sleeping naked. She had slept naked her entire life, but he never made any advances towards her. They rarely talked because their waking hours were direct opposites.

Mattie woke up and saw Tamir lying next to her naked. She had a feeling in her loins that she had never experienced before. She carefully reached over and slowing stroked his manhood causing it to harden in her hand. She heard him softly moaning as she was getting wetter and wetter. She rolled over onto him and slid him into her wetness. Because of the size of his appendage, she had to slowly take deeper and deeper. When she was finally able to get all of him inside her, she experienced her first orgasm and the feeling of her juices being released. As she continued to move up and down on the shaft, she had a second, then a third, and a fourth orgasm. She could see his teeth clenching telling her that he was holding back. That caused her to move up and down faster and harder which, in turn, sent stimulation into her. The sound of their flash smacking every time she pushed downward became louder and louder until Mattie heard Tamir grunt. She remained motionless as she felt the pulsations of his juices flowing up into her. When the pulsing stopped, Mattie rolled over and went to sleep. When she awoke an hour later, Tamir was sleeping soundly.

Mattie made dinner for her and Tamir and then he dressed and left to do business. She watched television until late in the evening and then scooped up Jameel and put him in his crib.

***

The briefing room at the police department had been reserved for the planning of the execution of a search warrant on the residence of a suspected drug dealer. The DEA sent a male and a female agent, the

Sheriff's Department sent two male Deputies and the Police Department had two male officers. The residence had been scoped out and the Task Force knew that the exterior door was unlocked. All of the officers donned raid jackets, which had large yellow lettering saying "POLICE" on the back of the jacket, and three of the officers signed out AR-15 tactical rifles. One of the City officers, who was large framed, was assigned the battering ram, which is a twelve pound metal bar to break the door down if the occupants refused to open it. They drove up to the address in two unmarked vans and walked in the unlocked door. The steps were angled in such a manner that placed the Task Force at a disadvantage. The officers slowly went up the steps until they were at the door. The second City officer banged on the wooden door and yelled, "POLICE, SEARCH WARRANT, OPEN THE DOOR!" When there was no response, the officer with the ram took the lead and hit the door at the center locking mechanism. The twelve pound ram barely put a dent in the door.

***

Mattie had just gotten into a comfortable sleep when she thought she heard a sound coming from the other room. She was groggy and just rolled over and went back to sleep. Then she heard a second thud and became scared. She reached over to the night table and grabbed her cell phone to call the police. The woman answered the call with "9-1-1, what is your emergency?" In a whisper Mattie said, "I live at 7 West Main Street and I think someone is trying to break into my apartment." The dispatcher said, "Can you please stay on the line for about one minute, ma'am?"

The dispatcher called on the radio to the Task Force officers. She said, "I have a female on the phone at the address you are at stating that someone is breaking into her apartment." One of the City cops told the dispatcher to have the woman open the door" The dispatcher came back on the phone line and said, "What is your name?" Mattie answered, "Mattie Williams." The dispatcher said, "Mattie, it is the police that are outside your door and they need you to open it for them. Mattie told the dispatcher, "I am in bed naked and I need to put clothes on and get my baby out of his crib. I will open the door in just a minute."

Mattie put on a robe and grabbed the baby and put him on the couch, then released the electronic lock and opened the door. The officers pushed past her and searched the two rooms with their guns at the ready. They ordered Mattie to sit on the couch. When they were sure there was no one else present, they handed Mattie the search warrant and said they were looking for drugs. All the noise woke Jameel, who started crying. Mattie opened her robe to breast feed him showing that she was naked underneath. She made no attempt to cover up because she really didn't care what the men saw. The female DEA agent saw the men staring at Mattie's naked body and said, "Don't you guys have something you are supposed to do? I will watch her."

The men started their systematic search of the apartment. The other DEA agent came out of the bedroom and asked, "What is in the locked closet and where is the key?" Mattie looked directly into the agent's eyes and said, "I have no idea what is in that closet, I've never been inside of it." The City officer brought the ram in and this time the door crashed open with one swing.

They came out of the bedroom with a steel box that was on the floor of the closet. A deputy looked at Mattie and asked, "What is in this?" Mattie's eyes showed rage as she said, "What part of I have never been inside that closet got past your level of intelligence?" There was a glare of anger from the cop, but the female DEA agent said, "Do your job, I believe that this girl knows nothing."

The other DEA agent went back to the van to retrieve a pry bar and returned to the apartment where Mattie was covering the baby who had gone back to sleep. Her robe was still open and this time the female DEA agent kicked a deputy who was staring in the shin. The Deputy yelped and went back to searching the area. When they opened the box, they found one hundred dollar bills wrapped in ten thousand dollar wrappers. They pulled the stacks out and put them on the dining room table, they counted out one hundred and fifty thousand dollars in cash.

One of the City cops said, "I've seen enough, you are under arrest." The female DEA agent looked at the cop and said, "She is under arrest for what, Moron? Nothing can be tied to her so go play cop somewhere and leave this young girl alone." The three men continued their search, but no drugs were found and there was no more money. As they were preparing to leave, the female agent asked, "Do you know Tamir Logan, Mattie?" Mattie said, of course, he lives here." The agent said, "Well, he won't be home tonight since he was arrested for dealing drugs. He is being held in the County Jail on Federal charges and will appear in Court later this week." With that the cops left and Mattie locked the door behind them.

Mattie went back to bed, but was confused as to what was happening and couldn't sleep. The next afternoon there was a knock on the door. Mattie yelled through the door, "Who is it?" A male voice answered, "Tamir sent me." Mattie unlocked the door and opened it to see a black male with dreadlocks standing there. The male said, "Tamir sent us a message to make sure you have whatever you need. This is a cellphone that has a pre-programed number in it. If you need groceries or anything else, just hit dial and tell whoever answers what you need and it will be delivered. We don't know what is going to happen as Tamir won't go to Court until next week and there is no bond set to get him out of jail." He immediately turned around and walked down the steps and out the door.

Mattie sat around the apartment for the next month without knowing what was happening or what was in the short or long term future. She needed answers so she put the baby in the stroller and walked down to the County Jail. When she entered the facility, the deputy at the entrance looked at her and said, "I am sorry but you are not old enough to be in here." Mattie's eyes got the "look" and said, "Tamir Logan is my man and this is his baby. You cannot stop me from seeing him." The deputy called for a supervisor who ordered him to let Mattie visit with Tamir. Mattie had to carry the baby through the metal detector while another deputy searched the stroller. Mattie was escorted to a room with three glass windows and was told to sit in a chair and wait for Tamir to be brought out. Mattie saw Tamir enter through the window and sit down in the chair. Tamir pointed to the phone handset hanging on the wall and picked up the handset on his side.

Mattie spoke first saying, "Are you okay?" Tamir replied, "I'm fine, did my crew come and check on you?" Mattie said simply, "Yes, they have been bringing me groceries and baby supplies, and I thank you. What is gonna happen?" Tamir said, "The rent on the apartment is paid for a year. They've got me on a Federal beef and I am facing forty years in prison. They believe I am a high level dealer and want information to bargain my sentence. I can't predict what will happen in the future. My lawyer is trying to cut a deal for me. I have to be very careful as to what I say because they are listening to every word and everything is being tape recorded. I made sure to buy your favorite cereal before I got busted. I put it in the cabinet for you. Mattie said, "I will be back to see you again, take care of yourself in there." With that Tamir got up and left the room escorted by a deputy.

Mattie walked home trying to figure out what Tamir was talking about. She didn't like cereal. When she got back to the apartment, she immediately went to the kitchen cabinet and found the box of corn flakes on the shelf. She opened the box and looked inside. She saw a roll of bills stuffed into the box. She pulled the roll out and counted the one hundred hundred dollar bills. She put the roll back into the box and put it back on the shelf.

Three months had passed and Mattie was experiencing feelings that she had before. She called the number on the cell phone and told the man on the phone she believed she was pregnant with Tamir's baby. The man told her to do whatever she needed to do and they would deliver the cash she needed to do it.

Mattie called the clinic that had delivered her first baby and told them she believed she was pregnant and had the money to pay for whatever she needed. The clinic set up an appointment to verify her pregnancy and that, if she was in fact pregnant, the cost for it would be fifteen thousand dollars. She called the cell number and gave the man who answered the cost. The dude told her it would be delivered the next day. The next day a man appeared at the door with an envelope containing the cash she requested. The man also told her that Tamir wanted to see her.

She went to the jail and had the argument with a different deputy, but she ultimately was allowed into the visiting room. Tamir was brought out and said into the phone, "Are you really knocked up?" Mattie said, "I am having the same morning sickness as I did when I was pregnant with Jameel, but I have an appointment with the clinic to make sure next week. Tamir said, "The Feds are offering a twenty-five sentence if I plead guilty and guaranteeing a forty year sentence if I go to trial. Ain't no way I am going to skate on this one. Do whatever you need to do to get far away from me and this place after you have the baby. My crew will take care of you until then."

Mattie made all her clinic appointments and the baby came without a hitch. She named him Maleek. When the clinic asked the name of the father for the birth certificate, Mattie told them to put "Unknown."

Mattie was down to the last month of paid rent when she decided to follow Tamir's advice. She packed a single suitcase and a bag for the children. She laid the electronic key and the cell phone on the dining room table and placed the two boys in a double stroller and walked out the door. It was time for her to start a new life,

CHAPTER FOUR

Mattie walked to the Greyhound Bus station pushing the two boys in the stroller. She entered the bus station and walked up to the counter. Mattie asked the agent, "When is the next bus leaving and where is it going?" The agent looked up at the board and said, "The next bus leaves in fifteen minutes and ends in Cincinnati, Ohio." Mattie laid two one hundred dollar bills on the counter and said, "I need two seats."

Mattie boarded the bus headed to Cincinnati and sat in the front two seats so she would have her back to the other passengers to provide privacy so that she could breastfeed the boys. She placed the two boys on a seat and covered them with a blanket. She had made sure to bring plastic grocery bags and a can of Glade so that other passengers would not be inconvenienced when she changed diapers. She had snacks for her and Gerber baby food for Jameel packed and ready for the fourteen hour ride.

Mattie had absolutely no knowledge about Cincinnati, Ohio and that was fine with her. She wanted to start over with no baggage and build a life for her children.

Mattie was able to get short naps as the bus rolled north on the interstate highway. She would feed and change one baby at a time and then tuck the child under the blanket to go back to sleep. Both children remained quiet throughout the journey and Mattie was glad she didn't cause problems for the half full bus.

When the bus stopped in Memphis, Tennessee, Mattie asked the driver to please watch the children so she could quickly get some food. She bought six pieces of fried chicken because she could eat it hot or cold.

The bus arrived at the terminal in downtown Cincinnati at nine o'clock in the morning. Mattie threw out her garbage and walked outside to a cool Ohio morning. She hailed a taxi and told the driver she needed to go to the Catholic Charities Office. When the driver asked for the address, Mattie said, "I have no idea." The cabbie called his dispatcher and got the address. It took about ten minutes to arrive there.

Mattie loaded the children into the stroller and walked in the main entrance. A young woman at the desk flashed a genuine smile that made Mattie feel a bit more comfortable. She asked, "How can we help you today." Mattie said, "I just got into Cincinnati less than an hour ago and have no place to stay." The secretary replied, "Let me check and see who is available to assist you. Please take a seat, it will probably be a couple of minutes."

About ten minutes later a door opened and a woman in her fifties came into the reception area. She also had a smile on her face and said, "My name is Maggie and I will try to help you. Can I ask what your name is?" Mattie answered, "Mattie Williams."

Mattie followed Maggie down a hallway and said, "Maybe we should talk in a conference room because my office is small and does not really have room for the stroller. Maggie pointed to a chair in the conference room and then sat down directly across from Mattie. She opened a folder with a blank legal pad to make notes and asked, "What can we do to help you Mattie?" Maggie said, "I just got off a bus from Mississippi with my two babies. I don't know anyone here and have no place to stay. Maggie asked, "Why did you want to leave Mississippi Mattie? Mattie was quiet for a moment and then said, "My youngest baby's daddy is in jail for dealing drugs. He said that he is going to accept a deal for a twenty-five year prison sentence and told me to get as far away from Mississippi as possible and start a new life."

Maggie looked at Mattie and asked, "I only have one more question for you Mattie, how old are you?" Mattie answered, "I'm seventeen." A pained look came over Maggie's face as she said, "Ohio law prohibits us from dealing with anyone under eighteen Mattie. Juveniles are under the jurisdiction of Ohio Job and Family Services. I have a lady that I work with there. Let me call her and see what we can do together."

Jennifer Ortega was sitting at her desk when the intercom announced, "Maggie from Catholic Charities is on line two for you." She picked up the phone and listened to Mattie's tale and said, "I am swamped with my caseload, but get her over here and I will see what I can do to help."

Maggie got Mattie and her children a ride in the Charities van. When she got to the office of OJFS, Jennifer was waiting in the reception area for her. She led Mattie back to her office and pointed to a chair. Jennifer said, "Mattie, because of your age, I had to call a Juvenile Judge to see what we can legally do. He told me that because you are alone with two children, he would deem you as emancipated and we can help you." Mattie asked, "I am sorry, but I do not know what emancipated means." Jennifer smiled and said, "It means we can treat you as if you were an adult Mattie."

Jennifer said, "The first thing we need to do is get you some lodging arrangements. We have an agreement with a local motel to house you and your children for a few days. Catholic Charities will now be able to be involved and they will be able to arrange for food and needs for your babies. Let me get the ball rolling and we will have you in a room in a couple of hours. Until then, we have a reception area where you can get a sandwich for yourself and feed and change your babies."

Catholic Charities sent their van to pick Mattie up and took the family to a small motel and got them settled in. The charity delivered a large crib for the two boys and brought baby food to get her through their short term needs.

Three days later, Mattie was in the room when Jennifer knocked on the door. She told Mattie that housing was found and that Catholic Charities was scrambling around to locate furnishings for the two bedroom apartment in public housing. OJFS would be getting her Aid to Dependent Children and some kind of financial stipend to carry her over.

It took three more days for the apartment to be furnished. The charity van drove her to her new home. Mattie was notified that her children were eligible for a full day program through Early Head Start, a federally funded daycare learning program. She would take the children to the center for the six hour day four days a week where they received breakfast, lunch and a snack each day. When Jameel turned three, he was transferred into the Head Start program, and Maleek followed the next year. When it came time to start school, Mattie would walk the children to the school and be waiting outside for them at the end of the day.

Mattie made sure that the two boys took education seriously as they grew older. She would read to them and teach them addition and subtraction in the evenings. They were allowed to play outside for one hour and then had to do school work while she prepared their dinner

When the boys grew old enough Mattie directed them to the local Boys and Girls club. There was a room with computers and a place they could do their homework and play until their six o'clock time to be home for dinner.

With Jameel's grade point average, Mattie was able to secure a scholarship to nearby Roger Bacon High School, an inner city Catholic School. Maleek was in eighth grade so he would be at the club when Jameel would get off the bus. The boys were able to make friends and play after school and had a place to go on the weekends.

Maleek was busy doing homework when he looked up to see a uniformed Cincinnati cop walk in the door. The tall muscular cop stopped at every person he passed and chatted for a moment before moving on. When he got to Maleek, he stopped and said, "Hello, my name is David Vesper, what's your's?" Maleek stood up and extended his hand out and replied, "My name is Maleek Williams, sir." The officer sat down across from Maleek and said, "You are tall and have a muscular frame, do you play sports?" Maleek answered, "No sir, I just never got into it?" Vesper said, "I played professional football before I became a cop. Do you think you would like to learn to play football?" Maleek smiled and said, "I would very much like that, sir." Vesper said, I am off tomorrow, how about we meet here at ten in the morning and practice out in the parking lot?" When Maleek answered, "I like that, sir," Vesper got up from the chair and moved on to the next person.

Over the next several weeks the two would spend a couple of hours practicing football. Vesper taught Maleek to throw and catch the football and then showed him how to run routes as a receiver. As the summer came to a close, Vesper gave Maleek a pair of black gloves that he wore when he played for the Cincinnati Bengals professional football team.

Mattie was able to get Maleek a scholarship to Roger Bacon as well. The catch was that the boys had to work at the school cleaning rooms and sweeping the halls to earn the free tuition. Maleek was sweeping a hall when he looked at a bulletin board and saw that the freshman football team was having tryouts the next week.

Maleek went home and told his mother who dropped what she was doing and took him to a sporting goods store and bought him football cleats and warm-up clothes. Mattie laid two one hundred dollar bills on the counter to pay. It was from the money she had received from Tamir years earlier. Maleek was shocked because he had never seen a bill of that denomination before.

It was now five days before school was scheduled to start. Maleek and Jameel had completed their cleaning duties and Maleek asked if Jameel was coming to the tryout. Jameel said he would rather go the boys club and left to catch his bus. Maleek changed into his new clothes and carried the new shoes to the football stadium. The coach looked at the boys hoping to make the team and said, "Pick what position you would like to play and go to the marked area for that position. There is a quarterback, running back, wide receiver, offensive line, defensive line, and cornerbacks and safetys with a coach to evaluate you." Maleek went to the receiver section and watched as others were run through drills to measure their skill level. When it was Maleek's turn, he was told to run a cut route up the sideline and turn inward. Maleek made the catches look so easy that the assistant coach was getting embarrassed. The coach told him to take off downfield and purposely overthrew the pass. Maleek made a one handed catch of the pass without missing a step. The coach threw the next pass low, then one high, and the next one behind Maleek, but he caught all of them with ease. The head coach and the prospective players had all stopped what they were doing to watch Maleek in action. Every time Maleek caught a ball, he would return to the starting point and toss the ball back to the coach.

The head coach called Maleek over and said, "I've had the opportunity to see you in action and you clearly are not freshman team level." The coach saw Maleek's jaw drop and the sad look on his face when he said, "Be back here tomorrow to practice with the varsity team."

Maleek was on cloud nine when he jumped off the bus in front of his home. He threw the door open to tell his mother the great news, but she was busy putting ice on Jameel's face. Mattie looked up at Maleek and said, "Jameel got off the bus and got jumped by gang members because he refused to join the gang. He will not be returning to school until it opens and you two boys need to stay together at all times."

Maleek went to the varsity practice alone. The quarterback, who was in his senior year and was the star of the team, felt he was being upstaged by the freshman, and threw passes he knew could not be caught. Somehow Maleek caught every one of them. The varsity coach told everyone that Maleek would be starting at wide receiver for the upcoming year.

***

Jameel's swelling had gone down far enough that he was able to start school on the third day of classes. The two boys were walking to the bus stop when they saw three gang bangers walking toward them. One was carrying a metal pipe, one had an aluminum softball bat and the third had a rope with knots tied in it. Jameel turned and ran back toward his apartment. Maleek stopped for a second and then tan full speed toward the three thugs. He hit the punk with the pipe across the bridge of his nose, breaking it. He hit the one with the bat with a forearm to the jaw breaking it. The little punk with the rope dropped the rope and turned and ran. Jameel came walking back up just as the bus arrived to pick them up.

The two boys climbed onto the municipal bus as the driver looked out at the two unconscious punks. The driver grabbed the telephone handset and looked at Maleek and asked, "What the hell happened here?" Maleek, without batting an eye, said, "These two players decided to duke it out and knocked their ugly asses out. Someone has already called the POlice and they should be here shortly." The driver shrugged his shoulders and hung up the phone and pulled away from the curb. It was an hour and a half later when someone actually did call the police. Both gang members were transported to the hospital.

The gang called itself the Tot Lot Posse, named after a children's play area that the gang called home. They were in control of the streets surrounding the project and dealt the drugs.

The senior members of the Posse called an emergency meeting to discuss what action to take against the two boys who dissed them. The options were to kill them both or to declare them off limits and safe. The majority wanted both dead, but that would result in Cincinnati cops in droves breathing down their neck until all of them would be in prison. After a heated discussion, the gang made the decision to make them untouchable by the gang members. They could not afford the heat of the PoPo crawling up their ass.

The two boys left the apartment the next morning to get to the bus stop. As they were walking down the sidewalk they saw five bangers come out from between two buildings heading toward them. Jameel tried to turn and run again, but Maleek grabbed hold of his jacket preventing his escape. They were mere feet from the hood rats when the five separated leaving a space for the boys to pass. Maleek held on to his brother as they passed through the opening and continued to the bus stop. Maleek snuck a peek to see the five group back up and continue in the opposite direction. He now knew that the two would be safe.

Mattie and Jameel went to all of Maleek's home games. Even Officer Vesper showed up at a couple of the games to watch Maleek's progress. At the end of the season Maleek was named to the Cincinnati Enquirer's All City team as an honorable mention, a high recognition for a freshman player. As a sophomore, Maleek was named to the second team all-state and first team all-city. In his junior year he received first team all-state and was recognized by ESPN and one of the best players in the country.

Maleek and Mattie attended Jameel's graduation ceremony. Mattie bought Maleek a new suit and a dress shirt and tie for this very special occasion. Jameel decided that he did not want to attend college and accepted a job as an apprentice mechanic with a nearby Ford dealership.

Just prior to his final game as a Roger Bacon Spartan, Maleek was called into the coach's office. The coach told Maleek, "I have been receiving calls from college coaches from all over the country. They will be contacting you to meet and pitch their program. Have your mother with you and sit down with her to decide where you want to go to school. You will allowed to visit up to three campuses, so choose carefully. I am here if you need any advice or counsel, but you are mature and can make your own decision."

The coach was right as college coaches came in droves. Notre Dame, UCLA, Florida, Ohio State, University of Cincinnati, Michigan, University of Louisville and other programs came to his apartment to pitch what they had to offer. Maleek asked the same single question of each coach. He wanted to know about their criminal justice program.

Mattie and Maleek accepted the invitations of Notre Dame, University of Louisville, and the University of North Carolina as the campuses they wanted to visit. After a long discussion, Maleek decided to sign a letter of intent with North Carolina. The signing was filmed for the local news on all the television stations..

CHAPTER SIX

Mattie drove Maleek to the bus station for the eight hour ride to Chapel Hill, North Carolina. She packed him fried chicken and snacks for the ride. Maleek tried to take a nap on the bus, but his stomach was churning with excitement and his eyes would not stay closed.

After getting off the bus Maleek saw a man carrying a sign with his name on it. The man introduced himself as Willie Davis and said he was an Assistant Coach of the Tarheels football team. He grabbed Maleek's luggage and took him to a car. They drove to the dormitory that Maleek would be calling home for the next four years. He was introduced to his roommate, a running back named Danell Henry. The two formed a bond almost immediately that lasted until Henry graduated two years later.

Maleek was in his room when three of his teammates walked into the dorm room. They told him that there would be a team party and that his attendance was mandatory. It would be an opportunity for him to meet all his new teammates and for athletic boosters, who donate large sums of money to the program, to meet him.

Maleek walked into the hotel ballroom where the party was being held. There were a few hundred people in the room, almost none of them he knew. Henry, who was a junior, grabbed him by the arm and introduced him to offensive and defensive players, including the quarterback, who had aspirations to play pro ball after his graduation this year. Players walked up and tried to hand him alcohol which was flowing freely at the party. Most of the players who were drinking were not of legal age and were surprised when he declined and drank straight Pepsi. He was standing alone watching all of the goings-on when a pretty young blonde walked up to him. Without speaking a word, she unzipped his pants and dropped to her knees. Maleek was in total shock and unable to move or speak as she put his penis in her mouth. When she was done, she put his manhood back in his pants, zipped up his pants and walked away to a rousing round of applause. Maleek was embarrassed and had no clue what to do next. A defensive lineman walked up and said, "You've now been officially welcomed to the Tarheels team. We do that to all the newbies."

Maleek was sipping on his drink when a fat balding man with a large cigar stuck in his mouth walked up to him. The man said, "I am Darcy Clump and I am one of Carolina's biggest boosters. I own a car dealership on the north side of town and you need to come down so we can talk. Maleek chased down Danell and asked him what he should do. Danell told him to go see the man because it would go a long way with the coaches.

***

Maleek walked into the dealership and told a salesman that he wanted to see Mr. Clump. The salesman looked up into Maleek's eyes and asked, "Are you the hotshot wide receiver I keep hearing about?" Maleek blushed as he replied, "I don't know if I am a hotshot, that will be determined, but Mr. Clump asked me to stop in."

Clump meandered out of an office and shook Maleek's hand. He said, "I built this dealership up from nothing and I have always been a big fan of

North Carolina football. Come with me, I want to show you something." They walked out into the back lot and Clump pointed to a white nineteen seventy-seven Cadillac convertible sitting on the lot. Clump said, "I want you to have this. I will take care of the license plates and title and it will be ready for you tomorrow." Maleek asked, "Isn't that a violation of NCAA rules that could get me banned from playing?" Clump laughed hard and said, "I know all of the rules and you will work for me to pay it off. You will come to sales area and talk to the customers about football. As you get more and more known as a star player, it will draw people here who will buy cars from me. It is simply good business."

***

Maleek found out that the world of college football is a universe apart from high school. There were two a day practice sessions with coaches screaming obscenities. Then there was the physical training regimen, followed by watching hours of video of both the next opponent and individual practice performances.

In between attending classes and practice, Maleek would focus his total attention on studying. Many of the players would party, but Maleek would stay in the room trying to learn, just as his mother had trained him. He owed her to work as hard as he could to get his education.

The first game of the season was against conference foe Clemson University. Located nearby, this was a rivalry that drew a large contingent of fans from South Carolina. To make things worse, Clemson was voted the pre-season number one in the country. In the locker room pre-game, the head coach railed about the importance to the Tarheel faithful to bring home this win.

Clemson lost the coin toss and kicked off to North Carolina. The first play from scrimmage was a pass route for Maleek. He would go two yards from the line and cut left into the area in between the zone coverage. The ball was already in the air when Maleek made the cut. It hit him in the chest and he immediately turned downfield. He did even see the cornerback who hit him blindside and rang his bell. Welcome to the world of college football Maleek. He was just happy he did not drop the ball.

The score at the end of the first quarter was Clemson 3-NC 0. The quarterback told Maleek the ball would be over his left shoulder on a long pass. Maleek faked moving left at took off at full speed. The ball arrived at the same time Maleek arrived and he only had one person between him and the end zone. Maleek faked left freezing the defender for a split second and opened the after-burners to the end zone. He flipped the ball to the official as three of his own players tackled him in joy. North Carolina lost the game 27-10, but the coach did not scream at Maleek

Maleek's classes took him deep into the world of crime and punishment. He listened intently as the professors tried to explain the operation of the police, courts, and corrections.

Maleek's second college game earned him a top ten on ESPN, Carolina had the ball on the Kentucky fourteen yard line and the qb called a pass. The throw was wild and Maleek had to fully extend and was in the air when he made the catch. North Carolina won the game 10-7.

The weeks of games and classes flew by. North Carolina ended the season at 6 wins and 8 losses and did not get a bowl bid. Maleek continued to make his obligatory appearances at the car dealership to schmooze with the customers to pay off the debt of the car.

At the end of the school year, Maleek drove back to Cincinnati to spend two weeks with his mother. He learned that Jameel was doing well at the Ford dealership and was a full mechanic. Jameel was getting married to a woman who worked there as a secretary. After the visit, Maleek returned to Chapel Hill and worked the summer at the dealership.

In his sophomore year, Maleek was named Player of the Week in the Atlantic Coast Conference, but the season was disappointing in the win-loss column. At the end of the season, the head coach was fired. Maleek was introduced to the new head coach and was told that the offense would be built around him in his junior year. The team had a new quarterback who could throw a football sixty yards in the air.

Maleek really did not attempt to make friends at school. He was too busy focusing on his education, which showed in his 3.8 gpa, and staying in shape for football. A red headed cheerleader made numerous attempts to woo him, but he didn't have time for a woman in his life at this time.

His junior year was more successful for the team. It ended with a record of 8 wins-6 losses and Maleek caught seventeen touchdown passes. The team made it to a bowl game, but lost 27-24 on a last second field goal by nationally ranked Oklahoma State.

He stayed in Chapel Hill picking up summer programs and got the opportunity to intern with the Charlotte, North Carolina Police Department. He was never made a sworn officer, but was given college credit for his time on the job. He got a chance to follow cases from arrest to prosecution to incarceration. He was able to interview offenders and learn from them things that rang true in his own life. With the extra credit he obtained, he was a graduate student for his final year of eligibility.

Maleek's focus changed in his last year of football. He was ready for the year to come to a close and focus on his desire of a career in law enforcement. There was a knock on his dorm room door and two men in business suits were at the door. They told Maleek that they were considering him for a position as an investigator with the Department of Homeland Security. The interview lasted just over two hours. When they asked Maleek to tell them about his life, Maleek paused for a full two minutes before giving them an answer. "I am where I am today because of two people. My mother, who made me toe the line, and a Cincinnati police officer who was the father I never had. I have never seen or met my real father. My mother told me he went to Federal Prison for dealing drugs, so the Cincinnati cop became a surrogate father, teaching me how to play football and how to be a good person. I have been committed into getting a good education and I made the right decision coming here.

One of the investigators asked, "What about the NFL? It is my understanding that you are good enough to play at that level. Maleek said, "I will definitely be watching the draft on television, but I don't believe that I will be drafted. I can go to the Combine in

Indianapolis to be seen by the scouts, but I think I will
be focusing my attention on my career in law
enforcement. The investigators thanked Maleek for
his time and left. A week later they were back offering
him a job contingent on his passing a background
investigation and completion of a training school.

***

Mattie made arrangement for her, Jameel and his
new wife to go to Chapel Hill for Maleek's graduation.
He would leave with a Masters Degree in Police
Administration and an overall 3.6 gpa.

Mattie was overwhelmed by the size of the graduating
class. Thirty-five hundred graduates filled the Dean
Smith Center, where the Tarheels play basketball.
The auditorium was filled with twenty thousand family
and friends.

CHAPTER SEVEN

Maleek had two weeks until he had to be in Washington, D.C. for his pre-employment testing with DHS. He decided that he wanted to spend his time at home in Cincinnati so Mattie decided to ride back with him and sent Jameel and his wife home. Mattie told Jameel she wanted to ride in what she called Maleek's "tank."

They could not have picked a more perfect May day for the ride home. They had bright sunlight as they marveled at the hills of North Carolina, Tennessee and Kentucky. His day was made when Mattie told him how proud she was of all his accomplishments and Maleek told his mother that is was HER who made him the man he is today.

They had just entered Ohio on Interstate 75 when it started to drizzle. Maleek had to pull over to the shoulder to put the top of the convertible up and he and Mattie were laughing about leaving a sunny perfect day and returning to that place called home.

The next day Maleek drove over to Roger Bacon High School to stop and see his coach. When he walked into the coach's office, he saw the shrine on the wall of his college career at North Carolina. There were pictures from North Carolina papers and a story done on Maleek in Sports Illustrated. The coach was sitting at his desk and didn't notice someone had entered. When he looked up and saw Maleek, The coach leaped out of his chair and ran around the desk to hug Maleek. The coach asked, "Do you think you have a chance in the upcoming NFL draft?" Maleek smiled and said, "Not really coach. I will be watching it, but I don't believe my career put me in the spotlight enough to catch the attention of the scouts. I had an offer to go to the NFL Combine in Indianapolis, but I got a job offer and have to be in Washington, D.C. in a couple of weeks. I just got back yesterday and wanted this to be my first stop. The coach grabbed Maleek and said, "Let's go down to the stadium. The team has voluntary workouts and I would like whoever is there to get the chance to meet you." There were several players in the workout room and they all looked in awe to meet a graduate of the school who played Division I college football.

***

Mattie made a special dinner so that Maleek could spend time with Jameel and his wife Marcy. It was at the dinner that Marcy announced that Mattie would be a grandmother almost causing Mattie to fall off the chair. That evening was the NFL draft on television and they all sat glued to the television to watch to see if Maleek would get drafted by a professional team. About forty-five minutes before the show was to start, there was a knock at the door. It was a crew from Local12 News who wanted to video him watching the show for the eleven o'clock news. Maleek had a sneaking suspicion that his high school coach had tipped them off. When he was not drafted, the reporter asked how disappointed Maleek was. Maleek said, "I got a college degree for playing football. It was not only a great experience, but I learned life skills that will take me forward."

***

Maleek went down the street to the Boys and Girls club where many of the employees were the same as when he was there as a kid. The employees took

Maleek around and introduced him to all the kids that were playing, lauding that he played college football at the highest level. Maleek finally caught up with his mentor Officer David Vesper. They met for lunch at a Frisch's Big Boy restaurant and Maleek bubbled over with excitement thanking Vesper for being his mentor and making him a successful football player. Vesper wanted to know if Maleek was heading to the Combine. Maleek answered, "No, I have not told anyone this yet, but I have a job offer to be an investigator with Department of Homeland Security and have to be in D.C. for the pre-employment testing end of next week."

Maleek spent the rest of his time at home just lounging. He packed a suitcase for this two day stay in D.C, but was surprised when his mother presented him with a new suit and tie for him to wear. He slowly drove up Interstate 71 passing through Columbus, Ohio, Wheeling West Virginia, Pittsburgh and Philadelphia, Pennsylvania. He was surprised when he drove through the tunnels on the Pennsylvania Turnpike and laughed at seeing the number of State Troopers writing traffic tickets on the toll road. When he finally pulled into the hotel that DHS had reserved for him, he was worn out from the ten hour drive, so he laid down to get a nap. When he woke up, he went to the hotel restaurant for dinner and then to the bar for a quick beer.

The bar was about half full and the big screen television was broadcasting the Senator Baseball team playing the Yankees. He was relaxing and slowly enjoying his beer when a brunette sat down next to him. She asked, "Are you a regular here?" Maleek answered, "No, I am here for two days for a job interview and then I return to my home in

Cincinnati." The woman said, "My name is Marcie and I work as a secretary for the Department of Agriculture. What kind of job are you applying for?" Maleek said I am applying for a government job too," and stopped there. Marcie said, "Are you at least going to buy me a drink?" Maleek looked at the bartender and said, "Put her drink on my tab." Marcie told Maleek about the crazy pace at which Washington functions and, after her second drink asked, "Are you staying at this hotel?" When Maleek said yes Marcie asked, "Are you going to invite me up to your room?" Maleek smiled and answered, "No, I am not. I have an early appointment, so I can't." Without saying another word, Marcie pushed her stool back and stormed away.

Maleek woke up early so he could get in a short run and have breakfast before the DHS car arrived to pick him up. His room phone rang and the caller said they were there to pick him up. Two men in business suits were in the front seat, so Maleek rode in the backseat. The driver took him down Pennsylvania Avenue passing the White House and the Capitol Building. Maleek was confused that the east-west streets were all single letter and the north-south streets were all numbers. With the exception of Pennsylvania Avenue of course.

The car pulled up at an older brick building with the words "UNITED STATES DEPARTMENT OF HOMELAND SECURITY" embedded into the brick. The passenger pointed to the door and said, "Good luck today. We will be back to pick you up when you are done." Maleek walked into a lobby area and immediately observed four lanes with armed officers and metal detectors that he would need to pass through. On the other side was a single desk with an armed officer seated with a computer. He approached the desk officer, who immediately asked for his driver's license and reason for being there. Maleek pulled out his license and a letter on DHS stationary telling him where and when to arrive. The desk officer pointed to a set of chairs and told Maleek he would have to wait for his escort to arrive. It took about five minutes for a young man in a suit to come and motion him to the desk. The officer handed Maleek a nametag with his picture on it. The officer told Maleek, "You will need to be wearing this the whole time that you are in the building, then return it when you leave."

The young man in the suit took Maleek to an elevator and punched the fourth floor button. The two walked down a hallway and his escort pointed toward a door saying, "This is the polygraph room.". Maleek opened the door and entered a waiting area. The young man said, "I will be here waiting for you when you are done. Enter that door on your left." Maleek opened that door and saw two chairs and a table in the room. There was a full glass wall showing a second room with two chairs and a desk with something sitting on the desk. The door behind him opened and a man in a worn shirt and tie walked in and sat down. "My name is Don Bergan and I conduct all the pre-employment polygraphs for DHS. I will explain the process to you so that there is no confusion and will, hopefully, allay your fears. The polygraph is conducted in three parts. The first part is the interview where we will talk about the questions you will asked on the machine. There are no ambiguous questions. Every question in part one of the polygraph examination will have a yes answer, and every question in the second part will have a no answer. The first part will give me a baseline reading as to how nervous you are and how you react to the question. Part two will be the questions I am required to ask of all applicants and any questions I may develop during our talk. I am neither here to be your friend nor your enemy. I am only here to assure you are telling the truth. Are you ready to get started?" Maleek nodded and Bergan pulled out a notebook. The interview portion lasted about an hour and a half, the polygraph itself took only fifteen minutes. When it was all done Bergan looked at Maleek and said, "I wish you well and thank you for your honesty."

Maleek walked out into the entry area and the young man was playing a game on his phone. The young man said, "Hope that it went well for you. DHS provides lunch to all of the applicants, so we will go down to the cafeteria before we move to the next stage.

***

The second phase was the psychological testing. Maleek was lead into a small room with a chair and a desk. On the desk was a booklet. The cover page was marked "Minnesota Multiphasic Personality Inventory". The receptionist told Maleek to carefully read the instructions before starting the test. She told him there was no timeline for the test, so he just needed to complete it. She also told him to go back and answer random questions when he was done and verify the same answer on the answer sheet. If the questions did not match, he would risk the test being skewed and potentially the loss of the job.

Maleek opened the booklet and read the instructions thoroughly. It said, "You will be give five hundred and forty multiple choice questions to answer. There are no right or wrong answers, but you will need to answer each question honestly, so read each carefully."

It took Maleek two and one-half hours to complete the test. He went back and verified random questions and they all matched, so he was comfortable. He took the answer sheet out to the receptionist and was told to have a seat for the Doctor. An Asian man in a white coat walked out and introduced himself as Dr. Dennis Choi. He told Maleek to follow him down the hall to a room. Dr. Choi asked Maleek what his perceptions of the MMPI were and Maleek said, "It seemed that some of the questions were redundant, just phrased differently." Dr. Choi just smiled and said, "Very perceptive. How would feel about having to carry a gun at work?" Maleek thought for a second and answered, "It would be just a tool for work, nothing more." The Dr. asked, "Do you think you could actually take a human life?" Maleek answered, "I do not believe anyone can really answer that question until they face it in reality. I would say that it would depend on the circumstances." When the interview was completed, Dr. Choi returned Maleek to the waiting area where his escort was patiently waiting.

The next stop was Human Resources. Maleek needed to complete an application for employment, waivers for educational, medical and employment information. The woman told Maleek that he had a conditional offer of employment with DHS, but that the offer would be contingent on him passing the background, polygraph and psychological testing. That process would take about two weeks. If he was hired, he would need to return to D.C. to be sworn and commissioned, receive firearm training and scheduled for training at the Federal Law Enforcement Training Center in Glynco, Georgia.

Once sworn in, Maleek would be paid for everything that he was required to do. The woman said that Maleek was covered for one more night at the hotel, or he could leave today. It was his choice.

His escort returned him to the lobby and a different desk officer took his visitor badge. The two DHS officers drove him back to his hotel where he spent the night.

CHAPTER EIGHT

Maleek returned home to await the decision. To occupy his time he decided to go to Roger Bacon and complete the paperwork to be a volunteer football coach. He would spend three hours every day teaching players how to play football. He taught the pass routes that he learned from Officer Vesper to the young men, but then took it one step further. He made each player defend against a pass play to learn what it was that they needed to look for when a receiver was running a pass route. When the receiver-defender made an interception, he would make the defender explain what it was that made him able to intercept the pass. The result was that when they went back to being a receiver, they took additional evasive action to confuse the defender.

Maleek also made it a point to volunteer at the Boys and Girls Club to give back to the kids what was given to him. He taught football at the former playground of the Tot Lot Posse, the leadership of which were serving long sentences in Federal Prison after a joint operation with the Alcohol, Tobacco and Firearms and the U. S. Attorney for the Southern District of Ohio. The playground was now a grass field that served as a good place to play football.

Maleek received the call on Thursday that he was accepted to join DHS. He would be reporting to the DHS office in D.C. on Monday to be sworn in as an investigator, then going through a week long orientation program involving spending time with the various divisions of the organization and completing basic weapon training.

Maleek packed his suitcase for the trip and left Cincinnati on Sunday afternoon for the ten hour drive to D.C. He arrived at the hotel in the early morning hours of Monday and got checked-in. decided to go for a run before being picked up by the DHS vehicle. When he finished the run, he showered, dressed up in his suit and had breakfast in the hotel restaurant in preparation for his first day of work.

When he passed through the metal detector at the entrance, he moved directly to the desk with his identification and employment letter in his hand. The officer made a call and told Maleek his escort was en route. Laughing, the desk officer said, "This will be the last time you will need an escort to get in."

His escort welcomed him to DHS and took him to Human Resources to complete all of the paperwork necessary for employees. Maleek completed forms to get his healthcare, dental and retirement benefits. He also had to sign a Confidentiality Agreement stating that he would not give out any sensitive information that he obtained from his employment.

Maleek was directed to the Agency Director's Office for the swearing-in ceremony. Maleek was told to raise his right hand and then administered his oath of office to swear that he would fully enforce the laws and support the Constitution of the United States of America. When Maleek answered "I do" he was issued a gold badge in a black case and welcomed into the DHS family.

The escort took Maleek to the Domestic Terrorism office where he wished Maleek a great career telling him, "You no longer require an escort, don't get nervous when you get lost in this building, I still do." He shook hands with Maleek and left him with the secretary in the office. Maleek was taken to a door marked, "EMPLOYEES ONLY" and by the Supervising Agent who said, "I am John Daley, no relation to the golfer. I will be showing you what we do and how we do it." The two went into a room with a wall size computer map of the U.S. with red dots pretty much everywhere on the map. Daley said, "The red dots indicate where there are ongoing investigations conducted by either the FBI or our investigators. As you can see, there are hundreds of dots covering every State." Daley clicked on a dot indicating Chicago, Illinois. The computer demanded a password to open the file. Daley entered his password and a file showing the name and address of the subject of the investigation. The narrative of the file showed communication between the subject and Middle East IP addresses. Daley looked at Maleek and said, "This is the starting point. This individual has been assigned to an Investigator in the Chicago office and we will determine whether or not to start surveillance on him after we determine he is a threat.

Daley took Maleek from office to office introducing him to the analysts in their cubicles working. Daley introduced Maleek to an older man seated at a desk telling Maleek, "This is Bill Brothers, he will be with you the rest of the day showing you what he does.

Maleek's second day of orientation was with the Threat Assessment Unit. He liked the fact that all he had to do at the entrance was flash his badge and identification to clear through the checkpoint. He did have to stop and ask the desk officer where he needed to go, which drew a chuckle from the officer. He was taken into the "War Room" where there was another computer map covering one whole wall. The supervising agent, Charles Hurst, told him the dots indicated the locations of major events, such as the Marathons, Sporting Events and large political rallies that were scheduled. Hurst told Maleek that this office worked with the regional offices, called Fusion Centers, were made up of Federal, State and Local Law Enforcement. Next Maleek was taken to the office of Transportation Security Services, whose responsibility was interstate transportation systems such as Amtrak and Airports. Last, he was shown the inner working of Immigrations and Customs as well as Border Patrol.

Day three, four and five was spent at the firing range where Makeek was taught how to fire the .40 caliber SigSauer handgun that he would be issued. The instructor told Maleek that this was just enough training to allow him to carry the firearm and that he would be fully trained at FLETC. At the conclusion of the training, Maleek was issued a firearm and holster to carry on his person. Maleek's last stop for the day was back at Human Resources where he was informed that he needed to report for training at FLETC on Monday morning at eight o'clock AM. He could stay in Washington and drive from there or head home and leave Cincinnati on Sunday. Maleek decided to spend the weekend in D.C. to actually see the sights.

CHAPTER NINE

Maleek left D.C. for the ride to Georgia. He travelled
south on Interstate 95 to South Carolina and then
drove west on Interstate 20 into Georgia.

It was just after two o'clock in the morning as he was
driving west on the empty Interstate listening to a 60s
and 70s radio station and immersed in the music.
Suddenly he saw a set of headlights closing in fast in
the same lane as he was driving. The car was on his
bumper when he saw red and blue lights flashing from
the grill of the car. Maleek looked at both mirrors
intently to identify that the car behind him really was a
police car, but there was nothing that he could see
that made it a real police vehicle. Maleek did not slow
down or speed up as he continued west on the
Interstate. The two vehicles travelled fifteen miles on
the Interstate with the blue lights flashing on the car
behind him. When Maleek reached the top of a hill he
saw a second set of headlights coming over a hill
about a mile behind. The second car was closing fast
and Maleek assumed that a marked cruiser had finally
caught up. The vehicle with the grill lights flashing fell
back and the arriving vehicle fell in behind activating
the overhead red and blue lights. Maleek immediately
turned on his right blinker and pulled over to the right
shoulder. As he was slowing down, he reached into
his back pocket and took out his badge and
identification, laying it on the dashboard. When he
came to a complete stop, Maleek laid his long arms
over the driver's door. Since the convertible top was
down, the officer would be able to easily view the
inside of the Cadillac.

Maleek saw the trooper approach with his hand on the butt of his gun. Maleek loudly said, "I AM A FEDERAL LAW ENFORCEMENT OFFICER AND I AM ARMED!" The trooper slowly approached and when he reached the driver door Maleek said, "I am slowly reaching for my badge and ID which is on the dashboard." Maleek slowly reached to the dashboard and opened his case showing the badge. He handed it to the trooper. The trooper looked at the badge and ID and said, "Give me one good reason that you did not pull over when the first cruiser lit you up?" Maleek looked directly into the eyes of the young cop and replied, "Ain't nothing on that car that says POlice and it is two AM on a deserted highway."

Maleek watched as the trooper went back to his cruiser where a uniformed Sergeant was standing and listened to the heated discussion between the two cops. He was unable to hear the words that were spoken, but could tell the old cop was angry. The young cop walked back to Maleek and said, "Very slowly but quickly drive away." As Maleek was pulling away, he saw the Sergeant jumping up and down and screaming at the young cop.

Maleek reached the entrance of the Federal Law Enforcement Training Center at five forty-five in the morning. Immediately after turning into the road, he saw a large sign telling drivers, 'NO UNATHORIZED VEHICLES BEYOND THIS POINT." A second sign told drivers, 'HAVE YOUR IDENTIFICATION AND AUTHORIZATION READY." There was a checkpoint with two uniformed officers wearing tactical gear and carrying automatic rifles. Maleek handed the officer his Ohio Driver's license and his acceptance letter from FLETC. The officer took the documents to a shack while the second officer stood guard. The officer returned and told Maleek, Follow this road to the end and make a left to the first road. Turn left at the next road and go to the second building. It will be marked as Building B which is where you will be staying. Maleek arrived at his destination and went about unloading the car. He walked in the entrance of the residence hall where he was greeted by a residence manager who took him to his second floor room. The room had two beds and two storage areas and looked exactly like his dorm room at UNC. Maleek unpacked and stored his clothes and then took a shower. When he was done he laid on the bed to relax from the long drive.

He was almost falling asleep when he heard the click of the door lock from being swiped with a card reader. He watched as a blonde man who had to duck to not hit his head on the door enter the room. Maleek jumped out of the bed as the new guy said, "Hello, I am Denny Childers. I guess we will be roomies." Maleek shook his hand and said, "I am Maleek Williams and how damn tall are you?" Denny laughed and answered, "Six-nine, I played basketball at the University of Virginia. Where did you play ball Maleek?" Maleek laughed and said, "I played football at the University of North Carolina.

Maleek watched as Denny stowed his gear and then the two went down to the lobby to get directions to the orientation. They walked down the road and entered the main entrance to the Center. There were twenty-four tables showing a letter of the last name. The two split up as there were lines at every table except the "Q" table which had one person. When it was Maleek's turn, he handed to male at the desk his

acceptance letter and his ID. Maleek was handed a
school identification card and directed to a room
where a continental breakfast was available. He was
told that he would be required to wear his
identification at all times while a student.

Maleek walked around the large room with tables of
Danish, donuts, bagels, cereal of different varieties,
assorted juices and coffee, tea and water. Maleek
made notice of the varied agencies represented on
the ID's of the students, most of which he had never
heard of. He saw tags of U.S. Park Police, U.S. Mint
Police, U.S. Capitol Police, FBI Police, Smithsonian
Police, U.S. Supreme Court Police, NASA Police
Border Patrol, ICE, U.S. Department of Agriculture
Police, Federal Reserve Police, Federal Protective
Services and U.S. Department of Energy Police.
When Denny found him, Maleek saw that Denny was
employed by the Internal Revenue Service.

A warning tone sounded in the room and someone
yelled, "That is a five minute warning. Move toward
the Auditorium." Maleek and Denny found chairs and
drank their coffees.

A man in a suit walked up onto the stage and up to
the microphone. He told everyone that they needed to
get seated. He looked out into the full room and said"

> "Good morning and welcome to the Federal
> Law Enforcement Training Center. You will be
> with us for the next sixteen weeks. My name is
> Frederick Cowans and I am the Executive
> Director of the Center. There are two hundred
> and forty people in this room. You will be
> divided into six groups of forty, but, rest
> assured, each of you will receive the same
> training. On the back of your student

identification card is a number to tell you what group you are assigned to.

We do not operate a democracy. You will have requirements that you have to meet. The next sixteen weeks will stress you to levels you have never known. Even those of you with military basic training are going to experience stresses you have never ever felt before. You will receive training in firearms, driving, tactical entry, emergency first aid, executive protection, and Federal Law. Your successful completion of this training will determine whether or not you remain employed at your agency. Our graduation rate is approximately seventy-five percent which means that it is likely that sixty of the people in this room will soon be unemployed. We are not here to be your friend or your enemy. We are here to provide you the training you need to perform the function of law enforcement and to survive.

You will be issued uniforms that you will be required to wear on this campus. You will issued a replica of a .40 caliber Sig Sauer and a holster which you will wear at all times other than when you are in your room. You will be challenged by instructors, and if you are not wearing it you will receive punishment which could include loss of privileges up to expulsion from the Center. These weapons fire paint balls should you have a situation where you are in danger. No matter where you are or the time of day, you may experience an emergency situation requiring you to be a law enforcement agent. We are training you about the real world.

Your weekends are yours. You can remain on campus, go home or go to the City. Keep in mind that, no matter where you are that you represent this Center and are governed by our Code of Conduct. Any foolish act can result in your expulsion from the program.

If you arrived here armed with a firearm, you will need to immediately report to the armory and surrender that weapon. It will be available for you when the training requires live weapons.

The instructors and staff of this facility are here to make you the best you can be. Do not be afraid to ask them questions or for help. Our job is not to make you a success, rather it is to give you the opportunity to succeed. Best wishes as you progress. Go directly to the table with the group that you will be assigned and pick up your complete schedule of training. Good luck to all of you."

CHAPTER TEN

Maleek had just dozed off while watching an episode of Gunsmoke when the phone in his bedroom rang. The female voice on the other end said, "This is the Cincinnati Police Communications Section. You have been requested to respond to 4580 Hamilton Avenue for an emergency removal of MS-13 gang graffiti on a cement wall. A police officer is there awaiting your arrival and will remain with you until the job is complete to provide for your safety. Maleek told the dispatcher it would be about an hour until he would arrive at the address and then hung up. He immediately called Jameel, who was watching television with his wife and told him to meet at the office for the job.

The two loaded the truck and hooked the air compressor to it and they drove to the address. They saw a marked police car in front of the wall waiting for them. Maleek unloaded a twelve foot step-ladder while Jameel hooked up the hose to the compressor and filled the blast pot with the slag. While they were getting ready, the officer walked up to them. The young African-American officer looked at Maleek and said, "My Sergeant told me that you used to be one of us." Maleek softly replied, "That is something I do not talk about, sorry." With that, the officer walked back to the cruiser and leaned against the grill of the car watching.

Maleek was about halfway through the wall when the blast pot stopped working. Knowing that it probably clogged, he climbed down the ladder and went toward the truck to clear the stoppage. Maleek saw a car slowly approaching and then saw the barrel of a rifle coming out of the window of the car. He immediately yelled "GUN" and tackled Jameel knocking him to the ground just as the bullets from the automatic weapon starting flying. Laying on the ground, Maleek looked back to the officer who was hiding behind the front end of the police car. He saw the officer jump up and begin firing at the car which was now speeding away and heard the officer scream into his radio, "5312, SHOTS FIRED, my location."

The officer ran over to the two laying on the sidewalk asking, "Everyone okay? Jameel was shaking uncontrollably, but Maleek was cool, calm and collected. He looked at the officer and asked, "How about you, are you hit?" The officer shook his head to indicate he was not. Sirens were coming from every direction and police cars were arriving in droves. A Lieutenant walked up and asked the officer, "Did anyone get hit?" The Lieutenant walked over to Maleek and told him, "We just captured the four bangers in the vehicle. The crime scene people need to collect evidence from here, but when they are done I would appreciate it if you would finish the removal. I will keep the street shutdown until you have completed the job. The City will pay for any damage to your vehicle or equipment."

The crime scene techs took pictures of the bullet-ridden wall and police car as well as collecting shell casings from the street. When they cleared the scene, Maleek finished the wall and the brothers went back to the office to clean up. Jameel was still a nervous wreck on the ride back.

***

There was a number 4 on the back of Maleek's identification card. He peeked over to Denny's card and was glad to see that he also had a 4. Maleek looked around the auditorium and saw a large sign that said "GROUP 4." Maleek and Denny walked over to the area and others began to group around a short man wearing military garb. Maleek thought that this guy looked exactly like the drill instructors he had seen on television.

The group formed in a semi-circle and the man said, "My name is James Bullock and I will be the group leader for your training. We will march everywhere we go because the key to survival in law enforcement is in discipline and teamwork. First, we will go to the procurement area where you will receive your uniforms and supplies. The Center will be providing everything you need except for your socks and underwear. You will then take the uniforms back to your dorm room to stow it. We understand that many of you arrived this morning and made long drives to get here, so you will be done for the day. We will group at 0700 every morning and I OWN you until 1700. I will be in charge of getting you to and from the cafeteria, getting you to training venues, and overseeing your exercise regimen."

He formed the group of thirty-four males and six females into two lines and they marched to an area where there were large boxes with their names written on them. Each box contained five gray golf shirts with the FLETC logo on the left breast, three pairs of gray dress slacks, one pair of shorts, one pair of dress shoes and one pair of running shoes. Maleek and Denny walked back to their dorm and unpacked the boxes. Maleek had to take his duty weapon to the armory to check it and then returned to get a much needed nap.

A loud horn sounded in the hallway of the residence hall at five-thirty in the morning jolting Maleek out of bed. A loud speaker announced, "GOOD MORNING CAMPERS, IT IS TIME TO START YOUR DAY." Maleek and Denny showered and dressed and went to the cafeteria for breakfast. Bullock was waiting for the group at the cafeteria and took them to a place that would become their meeting point every morning.

The first week was all classroom training teaching: The role and authority of Federal Law Enforcement Officers; and the United States Criminal Code.

Maleek was glad to see the weekend come. The Center had a bowling alley, game room and a movie theater for the students who remained on campus. The roommates showed their competitive drive as they bowled, played pool and ran both Saturday and Sunday.

The next three weeks were focused on weapons training for the recruits. They were taught how to accurately and quickly fire their duty handguns, shotgun and fully automatic tactical rifle. They were trained in Close Quarter Handgun which is where the officer and suspect are within three feet of each other.

Maleek decided to walk to the cafeteria about eight o'clock in the evening for a snack. He was walking toward the building when he saw a man and a woman arguing in the grass. The man slapped the woman in the face and she dropped to the ground. Without hesitation, Maleek ran full speed hitting the man in the chest with his shoulder, something he learned in tackling drills at Roger Bacon. Maleek heard the sirens of the FLETC Police cruisers arriving as the man lay on the ground writhing in pain. One of the officers grabbed up the female and took her to the clinic on the campus.

Maleek later learned that the female was the secretary to the Director and that the male was her ex-husband, who also worked on the campus. An instructor asked, "Why did you not draw your replica handgun?" Maleek thought for a moment and answered, "The male and female were not wearing blue instructor shirts and were not wearing face masks as they would if this were a staged event. Also, I heard the sound of his hand striking the female in the face and that made it very real. I just simply reacted after that."

Word of the incident spread like wildfire throughout the training recruits and people walked up to Maleek at breakfast thanking him for his quick and decisive action. Even Bullock gave him a compliment and told him to report to the Director's Office immediately after he was done eating.

Maleek walked into the office and the secretary jumped out of her chair and ran to hug him. The Director walked out of his office and said, "I just wanted to personally thank you for your bravery last night. I just sent an e-mail to the Director of Homeland to commend you for your bravery." Maleek walked out of the office walking on air.

CHAPTER ELEVEN

Maleek was looking forward to the day's training as he and Denny ate their breakfast. They would be involved in tactical training, but were clueless as what would face them.

They arrived at the classroom and were told they would be broken into five groups of eight to serve a search warrant. The suspects inside were believed to be planning a terrorist event and the house contained bomb making material.

The instructor told them they would need to choose a team leader among themselves. The group unanimously chose Maleek to be their leader. Each member of the group was given a folder containing the search warrant which contained the affidavit from the confidential informant and a diagram of the residence to be searched. The team was driven to the two story residence to develop a plan to safely enter and execute the warrant.

When they returned to the classroom they were told that the search warrant would be served after dark and that they needed to return at ten o'clock that night to serve the warrant.

Maleek tried to nap but his mind was racing with thoughts about the night to come and formulate a plan to keep his team safe. Denny told him not to worry because he had a team of brilliant people and they would work as a team to get it right.

At ten o'clock the team met at the classroom. Each recruit was issued a black tactical vest with the words, "FEDERAL AGENT" and under that the word

"POLICE" in white on both the front and back They were given fully automatic rifles which actually fired paint balls. The group formulated a plan which would have four agents enter the front door and four enter the rear door simultaneously. They also were given earwigs which would allow them to communicate with each other at all times.

They arrived at the residence in an unmarked black van. Maleek was driving the van and told his team to cover each other and make sure no team member got injured. He directed the four agents to the rear of the house and, when they were in position said simply, EXECUTE, EXECUTE, EXECUTE." They had been told that all entry doors would be unlocked and not to demolish the door because there would not be time to replace it for the next group.

Maleek, Denny, a female agent named Janice Worthy and an agent from the Department of Energy entered the front door as the rear team was entering the back door. Maleek yelled out, "FEDERAL AGENTS, SEARCH WARRANT" as soon he got inside the door. An instructor was in behind both teams with a go-pro camera to capture the event on video. One of the rear entry team spoke into the earwig, "One bogey down." Maleek pointed his hand upward and showed two fingers to indicate that the two agents behind him were responsible for the second floor. Maleek and Janice moved down the hallway until they reached a closed door. Janice bent low as Maleek opened the door where there was a male suspect inside. The male turned quickly and both Janice and Maleek fired, hitting the male in the side and chest. When he dropped to the floor, Maleek announced, "Second bogey down." The two completed the search of the front area and then moved towards the steps to the second level. The steps were in a square U shape and Maleek took the lead as they got into a single line moving upward. When they reached the last steps to the second level, Maleek lobbed a flash bang over the staircase. It exploded and almost immediately a male could be seen at the top of the steps with his hands above his head. The four got to the top of the steps and put the subject on the ground securing him with zip ties. Maleek, Janice and Denny moved down the hall to an open door and immediately saw a male with his thumb directly over a plunger and wearing what appeared to be a suicide vest.

Maleek signaled for the team to retreat and told them to take the suspect in custody down the stairs. Taking a position using the wall to protect him Maleek said, "Blowing yourself up is not going to accomplish anything other than to kill yourself, and that doesn't make much sense. Whatever you had planned simply ain't gonna happen, so please don't push that plunger." Maleek's eyes were totally focused on the man's thumb, and after several seconds, the thumb moved away from the trigger. At that point a loud horn sounded indicating that the exercise was over.

***

The group returned to the classroom where a large screen television had been placed in the room. The instructor smiled and said, "You will be the first to see the premier of your first movie". The group watched the entry into the front door from the go-pro and then saw the other team member making the rear entry. They then watched the event from the six cameras which were placed throughout the house.

The instructor said, "The entry was pretty much flawless, but I would have liked to have had flash bangs deployed as a distraction as you all made entry. You are the third group to complete the exercise and, so far, have had the best result. The first group made entry through the front door with all of their people and ended up in a foot chase when one suspect ran out the back. One student and a role player suffered injuries when the student tackled the suspect. The second group got blown up when the suspect on the second floor detonated the device he was wearing. All in all, you did a helluva good job. Class starts tomorrow at eight o'clock sharp."

The team left exchanging high-fives and complimenting Maleek on his leadership.

***

The group was told to meet in a parking lot for the first day of Executive Protection training. They arrived and were told that they would be doing several driving exercises to hone their skills for emergency driving.

The first drill Maleek ran through was in a specially equipped vehicle called the skid car. A Crown Victoria was encased in a form with wheels. The instructor seated in the passenger seat has the capability of lifting the vehicle off the ground rendering the steering and brakes totally ineffective. The driver loses all control of the vehicle.

Next, Maleek was required to do evasive driving which entails driving back and forth around pylons both forward and backward.

Maleek was taken to a location where a vehicle was parked in the center of a sand pit. He was told that he would be required to extract the vehicle from the sand. Luckily, he had overheard another group discussing this drill. They were saying that the only way to accomplish this was to rock the car back and forth and, while the vehicle is in motion, put the car in reverse and jam on the accelerator. While the car was rotating jam the car into drive and accelerate rapidly. Maleek was one of only four students in the group to extract the car from the sand. One of the instructors laughed at the number of times they had to use a winch to remove the vehicle from the sand after a student buried the wheels into the sand.

Next was a maneuver called the "J Turn". The student places the vehicle in reverse and rapidly accelerates rotating the steering wheel to the left and jams on the emergency brake causing the vehicle to rotate to the right. While the car is still rotating, the emergency brake is released and the vehicle drives away in the opposite direction.

The last exercise was the most dangerous of the day. It is called the "Parallel Intervention Technique" and is a method of stopping a vehicle in a pursuit. The PIT maneuver was done at fifty miles per hour and involves tapping the right front quarter of the pursuing vehicle against the left rear quarter of the pursued vehicle causing the vehicle being chased to rotate to the right and spinning out. All of the people in the vehicles were required to wear helmets because of the inherent danger of the maneuver.

The program was coming to its close and Maleek looked forward to his graduation. He called his mother to attend, but she declined because Jameel had just opened a new car repair center and would be unable to attend. She was afraid to fly and still did not possess a driver's license. She would, however, be able to watch the event on the internet and told

Maleek how proud she was of her youngest son. Maleek and Denny spent hours studying in their dorm room for the written examination that would be their last official act.

When Maleek was presented his certificate of completion at the graduation, there was an envelope with it carrying the insignia of DHS. When he returned to the dorm to pack, he opened the envelope and saw that he would have one week off and then he had to report to the DHS office in Minneapolis, Minnesota for his first assignment.

CHAPTER TWELVE

Maleek drove back to Cincinnati before making the drive to his new assignment. He arrived in downtown Minneapolis at nine o'clock in the morning. When he entered the building, Maleek was directed to a conference room where the SAIC and two senior intelligence officers were waiting.

Maleek sat down in a seat and a female said, "I am Special Agent in Charge Barbara Beauford and these are Senior Agents from my Intelligence Division. We are here to explain what your duties will be in this office. We have received intelligence that a segment of the Somalian community has been radicalized. The single tie of a number of the people we have arrested is they all attended the same Mosque. We need to get someone inside the Mosque to understand if there is a nexus to the radicalization coming out of there. We have set up an apartment for you in the neighborhood as well as gotten you employment outside of law enforcement to set up your cover. We have backstopped your new identity and want you to join the Mosque." Maleek waved his hand in the air stopping Beauford from talking. Maleek said, "Changing my name is a bad idea. My picture has been in Sports Illustrated and on ESPN. If someone recognizes me, I am a dead man. Besides, my real identity offers an in because of my sports accomplishments. The only thing that will need to be changed is my degree from UNC and removal of all law enforcement classes from the transcript." Maleek could see the two intelligence guys nodding their heads in agreement. Beauford nodded her head and told the two men to "make it happen."

Maleek drove to his new address and walked into the furnished apartment. Beauford told him that the hallway had been equipped with video surveillance but that, for his privacy, no audio or video was inside the apartment. There were numerous distress buttons placed throughout the apartment in case of an emergency.

The apartment was furnished in an Afrikaan motif. The carpet was red and the walls had African headdress and other symbols of African society. Maleek did not particularly like the way the apartment had been furnished, but knew that it was set up for a reason.

***

Maleek reported to his new job at D & K Advertising Agency the next morning. The business was named for the husband and wife team who created it and offered marketing concepts and assistance in media advertising. The owners were aware that Maleek was a Federal Agent working in an undercover capacity, but they would be paying his salary so that he would have a paycheck to show if he was challenged. The government would reimburse the business for Maleek's salary. The owners would be the only ones with knowledge of Maleek's real purpose.

The owners introduced Maleek to the staff and sent him out with another sales agent to meet with a bar owner about setting up a radio and television ad campaign. The owner was ecstatic to meet a real football star and mostly wanted to only discuss football, but ended up purchasing a package from the company.

***

Maleek was driving home from work when he saw red and blue lights flashing in the rear view mirror. He looked down at the speedometer and saw he was several miles under the posted speed limit, so he was confused. DHS ordered to him leave his identification and gun at the office, so he was defenseless. Two cops got out of the cruiser. The driver was black and approached the Caddy on the driver's side. The passenger was white and walked up the passenger side of Maleek's car. The officer stopped at the window and said, "Driver's license, registration and proof of insurance please."Maleek looked out the window and asked, "What did I do officer?" The cop got a scowl on his face and replied, "This is a high drug area and this car has Ohio license plates. This certainly looks like a pimpmobile doesn't it partner?" The white cop smiled and said, "Sure does." Maleek handed the requested documents to the cop, who then said, "Do you mind if we search your vehicle for drugs?" Maleek looked up and said, "Sure, as soon as you show me a warrant." The black cop looked pissed as he said, "Step out of the vehicle, please." Maleek asked, "Am I under arrest officer?" The cop answered, "Now you are, get out of the car"

Maleek was handcuffed and taken to the police station. When he was taken to an interview room, Maleek said, "I need to call my boss. Can you make the call for me? Call this number and ask for the SAIC of the Minneapolis office of DHS as I am a Federal Agent. I am sure she will want to call your Chief and have a nice discussion with her about the actions of her cops." The cops looked shocked and the white cop said, "Why didn't you tell us who you were when we stopped you?" Maleek answered, "Because DHS kept my ID since it is an undercover assignment."

The call to the Police Chief from the SAIC was less than friendly. When the SAIC was done screaming, the Chief told her Maleek would be returned to his vehicle with the apologies of the agency and that action would be forthcoming against the two cops.

***

Maleek had been in the City for two weeks when he decided it was time to go to the Mosque. He walked in the main entrance and told the first man he encountered, "I just moved here from Cincinnati, Ohio and am interested in converting to the Muslim religion. Is there anyone here I can talk to?" The man led Maleek to an office and introduced him to the Imam, the head of the Mosque.

Maleek introduced himself stating, "I have never been religious, but concluded that Islam might offer me something I am missing. This is the closest Mosque to my new home. I have only been here two weeks, so I am new to the area. The Imam listened patiently to the explanation then said, "We have had people come here in an attempt to infiltrate our ranks in an effort to investigate us, so don't mind my skepticism in your request. Without hesitation Maleek said, "You can verify who I say I am with little effort. People who are being deceitful would not come with their real identities. Check my name on the internet and you will find that I am very real. My football career at the University of North Carolina was well documented and my picture is everywhere online."

The Imam opened the internet and saw that what Maleek was saying was factual. They sat and talked about his football career and about the religion and its expectations. When they were done, the Imam took Maleek on a tour of the Mosque showing the areas

that were male only and the female area. Maleek
ended the visit with the statement, "You have given
me a lot to think about, let me think and come back."

***

Maleek was really enjoying his life in the business
world. He was developing relationships with business
owners who were really more interested in just being
with a renowned athlete. More than one owner
wanted Maleek to be the one being the spokesman in
the television commercial.

Maleek was ultimately allowed to join the Mosque. He
made sure to attend the Friday service and tried to
make friends with the other males at the Mosque.
Although people were friendly to Maleek, he felt like
an outsider without a way to reach the inner circle,
which is where he needed to be. He went so far as
inviting young men to his apartment and frequenting
the known hangouts of the young men without
success.

***

Months passed and Maleek felt like he was at the
place he started. He would meet weekly with his
handler, a man who emigrated from Iraq and was a
Muslim to provide an update of what he was doing
and to get ideas of what he needed to do to reach the
inner sanctum.

***

Maleek was sitting on the couch in his apartment
watching television when there was a knock at the
door. Maleek opened the door and saw two males
dressed in Muslim garb. One of the men pulled out a

gun and fired one shot hitting Maleek in the stomach. Maleek dropped to the floor and the two men ran. Maleek crawled to the closest panic button and pushed it. Within minutes the street was packed with Minneapolis Police cars and Federal agents. Maleek was taken to the Emergency Room and into surgery for the gunshot wound.

Mattie was sitting in her apartment when there was a knock on her door. She opened it to see a Cincinnati cop and a Catholic priest standing on the step. They entered and the priest said, "I am a police chaplain for the Cincinnati Police Department. Your son was shot earlier this evening in Minneapolis and underwent surgery for a wound to the stomach. The surgery was successful and the bullet did not hit anything vital. The doctors say that Maleek is expected to make a full recovery. Maleek sent a message that you do not need to go to him and that he will call you tomorrow." Mattie thanked the two men and they left."

Maleek did call his mother the next morning to convince her that he was okay. He was laying in the hospital bed watching a football game when a man walked into the room. Maleek looked up at the man and asked, "Do I know you?" The man looked at Maleek and said, "Yes, we met at the Mosque. I was sent by the Imam who wanted to make sure that you are okay." The two men chatted for a bit and then the man said, "We believe that the two men who went to your door last night believed that you are an undercover cop wanting to bust the Mosque." Maleek looked at the man and said, "I will tell you the same thing I told the Imam the first time we met. Undercover cops would not use their real name. So you know who shot me?" The man did not answer that specific question, but Maleek could read the man's face that he did know who shot him. The man wished Maleek a fast recovery and said that he would tell the Imam that Maleek was recovering.

***

Shortly after the man left SAIC Beauford walked into the hospital room. After exchanging pleasantries and asking how Maleek was doing she told Maleek, "I have decided to terminate this operation effective immediately.'Maleek replied, "Boss, I disagree with that decision because, from the visitor I just had, I think I have credibility now." Beauford smiled and said, "This is not open to negotiation. This operation is over."

Maleek stayed at the hospital for five days and then returned to the apartment for his recovery. The apartment now had twenty-four hour surveillance to make sure that Maleek remained safe. When he was up to it, Maleek returned to the office and handed the SAIC his resignation from DHS. The letter said, "Regrettably, this position did not fulfill my goals of being in law enforcement and it is time for me to move on toward other options. The staff of the Minneapolis office gave me all the support and encouragement that I could ask for but, in the final analysis, this position is not for me."

CHAPTER THIRTEEN

Maleek was both physically and mentally beaten up as he turned onto Dutch Colony Drive, knowing that he was finally home.

When he opened the door Mattie jumped off the couch and hugged him like she would never let go. It was actually painful on the recovering stomach wound, but Maleek kept it to himself.

He went to his bedroom and slept for the next twelve hours. When he awoke the first thing he did was to make a call to Officer Vesper to set up a lunch meeting so he could develop a plan for his future. Vesper told him, "The State of Ohio will match the training you received at FLETC against the Ohio curriculum and determine what courses you need to have to become Ohio certified. The catch is that the request will have to come from the police agency employing you. Apply for any police position you can find and go from there.

Maleek told Vesper, "I need to find a gym to get back into shape and help the recovery of the stomach wound. I have not been able to do any exercising in the last month." Vesper paused for a moment and said, "I still have contacts in the Bengals administration and I think I can get then to let you use their facilities if you are willing to sign a liability waiver."

After the lunch, Maleek drove to Roger Bacon High School to see about renewing his volunteer coach status now that he was in Cincinnati to stay. The Athletic Director told Maleek that the school was looking for a paid Junior Varsity football coach and offered him the position. Maleek accepted the new position.

***

Maleek applied for police jobs with several suburban police agencies and took the tests for three of them. He got offered part time police positions from two others, but declined them as he was looking for full time employment. He also applied for the lateral entry program with Cincinnati. Maleek received a conditional job offer with the City of Fairfield, Ohio, a sixty person department twenty miles north of Cincinnati. He was preparing to accept when Cincinnati called and made a conditional offer as well.

Maleek accepted the Cincinnati offer, which was contingent on his passing the physical, polygraph and psychological testing. At the physical examination, the doctor focused on any residual issues surrounding his shooting wound. After the exam, he told Maleek that he would clear him for duty as a police officer. The polygraph exam was simple and he easily passed it. The psychological examination focused on the aftermath of the shooting and how Maleek was dealing with the mental stressors associated with being a victim. Dr. Don told Maleek that he would report to the City that he had no concerns about his mental health. Cincinnati offered him a position in the next lateral entry class.

***

Cincinnati sent the training records from FLETC to the Ohio Peace Officer Training Commission, the standard bearer for law enforcement training in Ohio. The Commission determined that Maleek would need to attend forty hours on Ohio laws, sixteen hours in

Domestic Violence, and sixteen hours in Missing, Neglected and Abused Children before they would certify him as an Ohio Peace Officer.

Although the lateral entry training would not start for two months, Cincinnati had just started a recruit academy and Maleek would be able to get the state mandated training. Because of the City's own requirements, Maleek had to be employed in order to be eligible to attend. It was determined that Maleek would work as a civilian employee of the department until he completed the lateral entry training. He would work in the District answering the phone or in the Property Room filing evidence, or other functions that did not require a sworn employee.

***

There were sixteen people in the lateral entry class. They would be going through four weeks of training in Cincinnati Police policies and procedures, Cincinnati City ordinances, Taser, beanbag shotgun, ASP and PR-24 nightstick training.

The class had nine men and seven women, all of whom left other Ohio police departments and were already fully certified officers. Upon completion of the training, they would each be assigned to a Field Training Officer before being allowed to function on their own.

***

While some of the students who came from departments with lower standards were experiencing problems with the instructors, the FLETC experience endeared Maleek to the Academy staff. Understanding that these were all trained cops, the curriculum was different than what Maleek expected and the program ran smoothly.

Upon completion Maleek was assigned to District Five for his field training on the second shift. He was introduced to his FTO by the Sergeant at briefing. Known to the cops as Pappy, Frank Feldman had been a cop for forty-five years and was the oldest active member of the Police Department. Pappy became a legend when he got a radio call to respond to a fight at a restaurant and responded, "Car 502 okay, I will be there in about twenty minutes." The dispatcher responded, "Car 502, repeat?" Pappy answered, "Car 502 I can make it in nineteen minutes if I run real fast, my police car has not come in yet!"

Pappy shook Maleek's hand and said, "I ain't here to be your friend. I am here to evaluate your skill level. I know you came from the Feebies, but that don't make you a real cop. Keep your mouth shut and listen a lot and you and I will get along famously."

Maleek was shocked at the two rode up and down the streets of their beat and Pappy called everyone by name that they passed walking. Pappy told stories about the good old day of policing, when parents actually cared about their kids. Pappy said, "I remember when you saw a child walking the street at midnight, you smacked them on the ass with a nightstick and they went home. Do that now and the parents want you arrested. This is my neighborhood because it has been my beat for more than thirty years. The parents of the kids I see were the kids of parents I knew from this neighborhood."

Pappy was driving up the hill on Vine Street while Maleek was running license plates on the Mobile Digital Computer. He entered a plate and the screen immediately lit up that the car was stolen. As soon as Maleek activated the overhead lights on the cruiser, the stolen car accelerated and the chase was on. They traveled a few blocks and the driver of the stolen car opened the driver's door and jumped out leaving the car in gear. Maleek jumped out of the passenger side while the cruiser was still moving and took off after the running suspect. Maleek was in no hurry to catch up to the suspect knowing that the little twit would tire out. He stayed close enough that the suspect knew he was still being chased, but made no effort to close the gap. Maleek continued to update communications as they ran through yards and streets. The chase went into an alley and Maleek radioed the information to Communications. The suspect arrived at the end of the alley just in time to fly over the hood of the police car that just arrived. Pappy got out of the driver's door, looked at Maleek and said, "You gonna handcuff him or do I have to do all your work for you?"

For the next three weeks, Maleek listened to the war stories of the old cop and took in all of the wisdom that was being imparted. As phase one of the training program came to a close, Maleek asked, "Pappy, how come you never became a boss?" Pappy just laughed and said, "I love what I do so why would I want to screw that up. Most of the people up in the Ivory Tower are people who came to the job around the same time I did and they hate coming to work every day. I look forward to coming in and being with all the kiddie cops."

At the conclusion of their last shift Pappy said, "I will see you at the end and expect you to be a street-ready cop. Listen to what they all say, then remember what I have taught you. Do it their way so you get past them, but never forget that we serve the people, they don't serve us."

***

Makeek's second stint was at District Four working day shift. District Four serves the north end of the City. His FTO was a ten year veteran by the name of Darnell Mansure. Mansure did not shake hands with Maleek and did not speak a word until they were in the cruiser. Mansure told Maleek, "I dislike having a rider, I would much rather work alone. I don't want a partner, a recruit or a rider, but I like the hourly bump and the overtime I get every time I get a recruit. Here is the simple story. Keep your mouth shut and just sit out the four weeks and I will give you a satisfactory rating so you can move on to the next trainer. We have nothing in common and nothing to talk about."

There was not a word exchanged between the two and they did nothing but answer mundane radio calls. At the end of the shift, Maleek went home totally frustrated. On the second day they received a radio call to respond to a two car crash with no injuries. Even though they were only a few blocks away, Mansure slowly drove around in circles. When they pulled up behind the vehicles in the crash, Maleek activated the overhead lights and opened the door to get out. Mansure looked at Maleek and said, "You can stay in the car, I don't need any help." He got out of the car as a black man approached and Maleek heard Mansure say, "Aaron, what the fuck you doing?" The two talked for a bit and then Mansure returned to the cruiser. Maleek asked, "You know him?" Mansure replied, "Yea, he is a Cincinnati cop. Go write the female in his car a ticket for Assured Clear Distance and then we will take her down to the Clerk's Office to pay it out." Maleek started to protest when Mansure glared and said, "Just go fucking do it!" Maleek got the female's driver's license and wrote the citation as he was ordered. She parked the Cadillac at the curb and the two cops drove her downtown to the Clerk of Court. Mansure grabbed the ticket off the dash and told Maleek, "Just wait in the car." A few minutes later the two returned to the cruiser and Mansure drove back to the car where they found the off-duty cop sleeping in the passenger seat. Maleek went home and considered calling in sick, but decided that he needed to keep his mouth shut and get through the two days before his regular off days.

After a tough four days of riding with a zombie, Maleek considered asking the supervisor to change his FTO. Instead he called David Vesper to get advice from someone he trusted. Vesper was silent on the phone after hearing the story and then said, "Maleek, I understand the frustration and anger that you are experiencing, but if you go to a boss, the story will be Citywide in every Police District within the hour and that will follow you around for years to come. If you can, you need to suck-it-up and get through the four weeks and put him in your rearview mirror. You already learned a major lesson from this moron. That is what not to do."

The next two weeks were a living hell for Maleek. At the end of each shift he had to stifle the urge to shove Mansure into the trunk of the cruiser and back it into a cement wall. The only release valves that kept Maleek sane were coaching football and having access to the Bengals training room. Maleek would go home and eat his dinner and then sleep through the night.

Maleek was now down to counting the hours before he would move onto the next stage of his training. He only had forty more hours of hell left. When he arrived at the District, the Sergeant told him to report to the Lieutenant's office immediately. Maleek knocked on the door and was motioned to enter. The Lieutenant said, "You will not be working the street today. You need to follow me." The two got into an unmarked car and drove to an office building on Eighth Street just west of downtown. They walked into the building passing a security guard at a desk and went up the elevator to the second level and through an unmarked door into a waiting area. The Lieutenant told the receptionist, "I have Officer Williams."

A man in a suit came out of an inner door. He extended his hand to Maleek and said, "My name is Sergeant Ken Roof and I am with the Integrity Unit of the Police Department. Follow me please." They walked down a hall and into a room with a desk and three chairs. Sgt. Roof pointed to a chair for Maleek to sit and went to the other side of the desk. Roof said, "I have a Form 26 for you to read and sign. I will explain it to you as you read it. This is a Garrity warning form telling you that you are the subject of an official investigation. You are required to truthfully and fully answer any questions that are asked. If you refuse to answer or are untruthful, you will be terminated from your employment immediately. Do you understand what you just read?" Maleek nodded and Roof continued, "We have no reason to believe, at this point, that you did anything wrong, but your status as a probationary employee puts your job in serious jeopardy if you are not completely honest with us. Nothing that you say in this interview can be used should criminal charges result from our investigation.

You also have the right to have an FOP representative or an attorney present should you choose. Please sign the form in the bottom right corner and we can get started." Maleek inked his signature and Roof said, "This interview will be recorded with both audio and video. We are conducting an investigation into conduct involving you and Officer Mansure. Let's get started." Maleek saw red lights come on with the two cameras in the room and was beginning to get very nervous since he was clueless as to what he could have done. Roof asked:

Q. Do you remember responding to a two vehicle auto accident on Montgomery Road at Kennedy Avenue?

A. Yes sir

Q. Tell me what you remember

A. Officer Mansure was driving. We arrived behind a Cadillac that rear-ended a Ford Explorer. Officer Mansure told me to stay in the car and he would handle the call. He met a black male in the front of the cruiser and called the guy by name.

Q. Did you issue a traffic citation to a female in the crash?

A. Yes sir

Q. Did you see her operating the vehicle?

A. I did not see anyone operating either vehicle. Both vehicles were stationary when we arrived.

Q. Then why did you issue the traffic citation to the female?

A. Because I was ordered to by Officer Mansure.

Q. At what point did you learn that the owner of the Cadillac was also a Cincinnati police officer?

A. I asked Officer Mansure if he knew the black male. He told me that the guy was also a Cincinnati cop.

Q. Okay, what happened next?

A. Officer Mansure told me we would be driving the female to the Clerk's Office to pay out the citation. When we arrived at the Clerk's Office, he told me to wait in the car. The two returned and we drove the woman back to the crash scene. The male was sleeping in the passenger seat and the woman drove away because the Cadillac was still drivable.

Sgt. Roof said, "That is all the information that we need at the moment. You will not be returning to District Four, but will move on to your next step in the FTO process. I recommend that you have no contact with Officer Mansure while this investigation is still in progress. Good luck with your career."

CHAPTER FOURTEEN

Maleek reported for his first shift with his new FTO at District Two, which covers the eastern side of Cincinnati. His trainer, Lee O'Neal, had twenty-one years as a cop and greeted Maleek with a smile and a handshake. O'Neal said, "What happened to you is known all over the City. I will try to make your experience with me as pleasurable as possible and we will make the best of a bad situation." That response made Maleek sigh a breath of relief.

O'Neal said, "How about you drive and let's get this show on the road?" The two stopped for coffee and were slowing patrolling the street when they received a radio run of a shoplifter fighting with security at a Kroger grocery store. O'Neal said, "I know that you do not know the streets so I will get you there." They pulled into the parking lot when Maleek saw a white male punch another white male and run. He jumped out of the cruiser and started chasing the suspect. Again, he made no attempt to close the distance between them because he knew the runner would tire out before he did. Maleek made sure to check the street signs so that he could keep Communications updated as to where they were. After a little more than a mile, the suspect collapsed and was writhing in pain. Maleek walked up to the limp man and rolled him over to handcuff him as police cars were arriving in all directions. O'Neal walked up and asked, "Why the hell didn't you just catch up to this little punk?" Maleek smiled and replied, "Look at him and you will see that all of the fight is gone." O'Neal broke into a big grin and said, "I like that!"

O'Neal let Maleek drive every shift telling him, "I like being chauffeured." O'Neal gave Maleek an honest evaluation of every police action the two were involved in and Maleek was appreciative of that. He was really learning from this veteran.

The two officers had just completed a criminal damaging report when a bank hold-up alarm came across the radio. They jumped into the car and O'Neal said, "I will tell you where to turn to get there, let's rock. Turn left at the second light. Turn right at the third light. The bank is on your left about three blocks away" The radio cracked with a vehicle description and both cops saw the car at the same time. Maleek quickly turned the cruiser around while O'Neal activated the lights and sirens. While Maleek drove, O'Neal was updating Communications. Maleek told O'Neal, I learned the PIT maneuver at FLETC. Are we allowed to use it?" O'Neal laughed out loud and replied, "Son, this is Cincinnati, we ain't allowed to put dings in the police cars." The pursuit moved onto Interstate 71 north and out of the City limits. The Sheriff's Department and the City of Madeira joined in and O'Neal said, "Let the County unit take over the lead and we will just stay in for the ride." The suspect got off the Interstate and moved down residential streets in Madeira. The driver made his mistake when he turned down a dead end street, but tried driving through the grass of a front yard. Maleek blocked his exit and the chase ended peacefully. When they were returning to the City, O'Neal said, "Ya done good rookie, handled it better than I could have."

With each shift Maleek felt more and more comfortable in the job. Maleek and O'Neal were sitting in a Frisch's restaurant having lunch when O'Neal said, "You go back to Pappy for the final stage, right?"

Maleek nodded and O'Neal continued, "Pappy is a trip. It is said that he buys a new car every eighteen months so he can keep a loan with the police credit union. That way he doesn't have to retire. He wants to die sitting in the cruiser wearing a smile."

As the last shift with O"Neal was coming to an end, O'Neal said, "You will do well in this business Maleek. You have the patience to allow situations to develop and that is something no one can teach. Your judgment is excellent and not much seems to flap you. If I can ever be of any help to you, please don't hesitate to call."

***

Maleek did not wear his uniform to or from work because he feared retaliation against his mother if the residents of the project found out he was a cop. He would drop off his uniforms at a dry cleaner and place them in his locker at the District.

Maleek decided to take Mattie out and find her a house. They looked at several properties until they found one in the north end of the City in a neighborhood called College Hill. Maleek had saved as much as possible and was able to make a substantial down payment and they moved her into her new home. The house had a nice back yard that she could plant a garden and had a large park directly behind it. Maleek and Jameel helped move everything into the new home and Mattie was as happy as Maleek had ever seen her.

***

Maleek reported to District Five for the final four weeks of his training. When he walked into the roll call room, he saw Pappy's face light up with a beaming smile. The officers working the shift all walked up to Maleek welcoming him back and making small talk. Clearly, they were all aware of the events that Maleek had gotten jammed-up with and wanted to show their support.

No sooner had they gotten into the cruiser, Pappy said, "I really love kiddie cops, they can get into crazy messes. Let's get you through this four weeks without getting either of us killed and you can go out and play a real policeman."

The four weeks blew by and it was time for Maleek to move on. On the final shift, Pappy took Maleek for a steak meal. He told Maleek, "Learn from everyone you come into contact with. Listen to their advice and contemplate it. Then use it in a way that best fits you and your personality. Don't try to be anyone but you."

CHAPTER FIFTEEN

Maleek received the note that he would be assigned to the Downtown District which serves the Central Business District. When he arrived for his first shift, he was told to report to the Captain's Office. Captain Jennifer Combs had been the Commander since the District had been separated from District One. She oversaw bike cops, the walking beats and the Special Events unit for downtown. The police station was across from Paul Brown stadium (home of the professional football Bengals) and Great American Ballpark (home of the Reds baseball team).

Captain Combs told Maleek he would be assigned to to the noon to midnight shift and would be riding a Segway, but that he needed to be trained to ride the two wheel motorized scooter. He would be reporting to the Police Academy for the next three days for that training.

The Segway is a totally silent motorized vehicle which can reach speeds of twenty-five miles per hour. It can drive on sidewalks or roadways and can fit into small alleys and navigate parking garages. She told him that she wanted him to be highly visible wherever crowds of people were. She him that he would be the visible face of the police department and that, the friendlier that he was, the better the image of the police department would be.

Maleek took the Captain's words to heart. He would park himself where there was a large number of people. This kept him in an area called The Banks, a cadre of bars and restaurants directly across from the professional sports stadiums. He would make it a

point to chat with the people outside and tried to
remain highly visible. He learned quickly that children
were especially intrigued by the scooter, but he was
told that he could not give rides to anyone. The pace
of downtown made the shifts go quickly. Knowing that
being able to navigate around stopped traffic allowed
him to respond quickly to any incident.

Maleek also enjoyed the ability to quietly sneak up on
dice games and scare the hell out of the players. He
was also able to catch marijuana smokers in the
parking garages. He was just having fun.

Maleek was riding on the sidewalk on Seventh Street
around three o'clock when he heard the sound of
moaning coming from an alley that ran from Sixth to
Seventh. He turned into the alley and was able to see
a man attempting to rape a woman next to the
dumpster. When he got close enough, he kicked the
man in the shoulder just as the man was trying to
penetrate the woman who was now naked from the
waist down. The male suspect rolled and scraped his
erect penis, crying out in pain. Maleek jumped off the
Segway kneeling on the man's back and getting him
cuffed. The woman was sobbing as Maleek called for
a life squad and cars for back-up. Police cars came
flying and a crowd stood on the sidewalks to watch
the chaos. Maleek kept his two hundred and twenty
ponds on the suspect's back as the man cried that his
dick hurt. When the medics arrived, Maleek ordered
them to place a blanket on the victim. Maleek picked
the suspect up off the ground and marched him onto
Seventh Street while the guy begged to let him zip up
his zipper, but Maleek said the world should see his
little wienie. The crowd was laughing as Maleek
turned him over to two cops at their cruiser. He told
the cops it was up to them whether they let the piece

of shit zip up, but that they probably needed to take him to the hospital for the injury to his pecker. Maleek returned to the victim and talked to her until the detectives arrived and she was also taken to the hospital. As she was being rolled to the ambulance, she looked at Maleek and mouthed, "THANK YOU!"

***

Once Maleek had six months on the job, he was eligible to work off duty details. These are security jobs approved by the City in uniform. Maleek loved working the Kroger grocery stores, especially the one near the University of Cincinnati campus where foot pursuits of shoplifters is an everyday occurrence. The beat cops would swarm the area whenever Maleek got into a chase because they knew he would wear the runner out and take all of the fight out of him. He also liked the downtown library because he could sit and read books and get paid for it. All of the money that he earned went to pay for his mother's house and he was paying it off quickly.

Maleek quietly went about his job and worked hard not to make any waves. He received glowing evaluations from the supervisors and was liked by the majority of cops. He had no use for the police union, but paid his dues because they were automatically deducted from his paycheck. He was also a member of the Sentinels, an organization representing the African-American members of the police department.

He remained focused on coaching football players and that kept him balanced.

***

Cincinnati was preparing for the professional All Star game coming in July. Other cities told Cincinnati that they had experienced a problem with out-of-town prostitutes moving into their City for the days leading up to the game. Captain Combs called Maleek into her office and told him that he was being detailed to the Vice Control Section to help them with a sting operation that they were developing. Maleek would be placed in a hotel room with a back-up team in an adjoining room who would be recording the solicitation of sex acts in exchange for money. Maleek was told to call escort service ads and make an appointment for the girls to come to his room.

Maleek showered and put on a robe to prepare for the night. He had his gun under his pillow and the five hundred dollars in hundred dollar bills spread out on the dresser. The first appointment was set for eight o'clock and then every thirty minutes after. There was a knock on the room door as Maleek was laying on the bed watching television. Four members of the Vice Unit were in the next room watching on video. Maleek opened the room door and looked at a six foot blonde woman who clearly could have had a career as a model. He stepped back and she walked into the room. Maleek pointed to the dresser and said, "Your money is on the table." The woman, who appeared to be in her early twenties, walked over and picked up the bills. Maleek said, "What does that get me?" The blonde walked over to Malleek and swung his robe open showing that he was naked under it. She grabbed his appendage as the adjoining room door flew open and the arrest team came in. The vice cops were laughing when they told Maleek, "Congratulations, your junk is now on video." Maleek

98

was blushing and retreated to the bathroom to put on underwear.

The second knock was a short redhead who looked to be in her late teens. She too picked up the bills and dropped to her knees grabbing his appendage. The back-up team flung the door open just as she put it in her mouth.

At the third knock, Maleek yelled, "Its open." Something about the person who walked in just did not look right. The skirt and pantyhose looked like there was a bulge in the groin area. The voice sounded very low for a female and Maleek put his hand under the pillow on his gun. When the escort grabbed the money, the vice cops came running into the room. They arrested the escort, who turned out to be a male.

At the end of the evening the vice cops thanked Maleek for the successful operation as all of the escorts were from hundreds of miles away.

***

Maleek was in the locker room getting dressed for work when the Lieutenant walked in and told Maleek that he would not be participating in roll call. He told Maleek to grab the Segway and report to the Lieutenant posted at Fountain Square. Fountain Square is the centerpiece of downtown Cincinnati. The Tyler Davidson Fountain was dedicated in 1871 and is in the center of the business district and the focal point of the downtown area surrounded by the central business district.

Maleek found the Lieutenant and was told to park the Segway behind the stage and take a position at the right side of the stage. The Sergeant told the ten cops that they were there for a protest to be held by a group called "Black Lives Matter." The Sergeant told the cops, "We will agree with absolutely nothing that this group has to spew, but we are here to protect their right to say it. We will be professional in our actions and ignore their trash talk."

Maleek listened to several speakers screaming out garbage about police abuses and how they kill black males. He reached his limit with a young African-American woman's disparaging remarks. He looked up to the stage and said loud enough that she could hear, "I am black, does my life matter?" The woman looked directly at Maleek and was having difficulty keeping her train of thought. What Maleek did not know was that a television news crew was standing behind him getting footage for the evening news and that the camera audio was on as well. The quote not only made local news, but was all over national network and cable news. It was seen and heard by viewers worldwide.

Maleek walked into work the next day and was immediately directed to the Captain's Office. Captain Combs looked at Maleek and said, "Have a seat officer. The Chief's office called me at six am to tell me they have received calls from *The Today Show, CBS This Morning, Good Morning America and FOX and Friends* all wanting you to appear on their shows to discuss the question you asked yesterday. The Department cannot stop you from accepting their offers, but it is in your best interest to find a place to hide until this subsides. Your days in the downtown district are over and you are being transferred to District Four effective this Sunday. Maleek replied, "I understand boss. Had I known that my question was being recorded, I never would have asked. I never saw the TV crew." Captain Combs smiled and said, "The question was valid and I respect that. If you ever need a recommendation, I am here for you."

When Maleek reported for work in his new assignment, the District Four Commander called him into the office. He told Maleek, "Mansure and the other cop had been indicted and fired, so you will not have to deal with them. That does not mean that their friends are going to like you. Just go out and do the job and they will come around." He was assigned to the daytime power shift from twelve noon until ten o'clock in the evening. The shift is designed to have cars on the streets to answer calls while the normal shifts are arriving or leaving.

***

Maleek signed up for his first Bengals game detail. It was a cold day in Cincinnati and Maleek had to dress in layers. The detail board showed that he would be working on the field on the visitor's side. He didn't even notice that the Bengals opponent would be the Carolina Panthers. The old cops were telling the story of the Bengals game in January, 1981, known as the "Freezer Bowl", where the wind chill was fifty-nine degrees below zero.

When the Panthers team came onto the field, Maleek struck up a conversation with Cam Newton, the Panthers quarterback. Maleek laughed and said, "I don't know who to root for since I played my college football at UNC." Newton asked his name and then said, "I have heard of you. You had a helluva career there. Why didn't you go pro?" Maleek smiled and answered, "I had hopes of being drafted, but when it didn't happen, I took a job offer out of college." Newton had to go out on the field but told Maleek,

"We will be in town until tomorrow. Pick a place and let's do dinner tonight. I'm buying."

Maleek met the quarterback at Ruth's Chris Steak House in the Banks area across from the stadium. They talked about their college careers and Newton's meteoric rise to the top of the National Football League. They agreed to keep in touch with each other.

***

Maleek was just riding around the campus of Xavier University when the radio cracked, "Shots fired, shots fired, Officer down, Bramble and Whetzel." Maleek was within four miles and hit the lights and siren. Driving down Madison Road, the main east-west drag, like a crazy man Maleek was going through intersections at seventy miles an hour. When he got to Bramble, he could see several police vehicles from multiple jurisdictions were there. He turned the cruiser sideways to close down the street to protect the crime scene. Even as far back as he was, he could see the dead cop in the street and the dead suspect. He saw grown men with tears in their eyes from the loss of a brother officer. Supervisor cars and fire vehicles went through a lawn to get around Maleek's police car and the media trucks were arriving as well. A Sergeant told Maleek not to allow the media hounds any closer than where his cruiser was parked. One cop who had visible tears in his eyes told Maleek that the dead cop was a twenty-six year veteran picking up overtime on his day off. The dead shooter was a seventeen year old kid who was capped by the second cop that arrived.

Maleek snapped to attention and saluted as the life squad removed the dead hero from the scene.

Maleek had never cried in his life that he could remember, but the tears flowed freely for a man he did not even know.

At the funeral home for the layout hundreds of people waited in line to pay their respects. When the father of the shooter showed up, cops there reacted angrily and forced him to leave. The man was later interviewed by the media and told them he was really sorry for what his son did and wanted only to pay his respects to the fallen officer.

The size of the crowd at the funeral was well beyond the capacity of Cincinnati's largest downtown church. Even though the officer was not Catholic, St. Peter in Chains Cathedral was chosen as the site for the service. Maleek stood on Plum Street along with hundreds of other officers throughout the service which featured statements by the Mayor and Police Chief espousing the impact this hero made on the Cincinnati community. Maleek saw uniformed cops from Australia, Canada and the United Kingdom as well as representatives of all fifty states. Maleek contemplated the fact that officers traveled hundreds of miles to pay respects to a brother who made the ultimate sacrifice.

The procession ran for seventeen miles and was carried live on all four local television stations. The route was lined on both sides of the street with people placing their hand over their heart or holding American flags. Maleek took in the magnitude of the event and came away with the belief that the majority of the community really was supporting of the job law enforcement does.

CHAPTER SIXTEEN

Maleek was a few days past his second anniversary of his being hired by the police department when he noticed a posting on the bulletin board of an upcoming Sergeant's test. His lateral entry status meant that his Federal time counted toward his seniority with the City and he met the three year minimum and was eligible to take the examination. Police Supervisors and even Captain Combs contacted him to suggest that he take the test because he demonstrated the leadership skills that the Police Department needed. Maleek went so far as to sign up for Library details so that he could study the required reading books for the examination. When the deadline for signing up passed without Maleek filing the paperwork, people all wanted to know why he decided to forgo the chance for advancement.

Maleek told everyone the same thing. He would say, "If I learned anything from Pappy Feldman, it was that he did not take promotion examinations because he did not want to lose his contact with the street. I did not understand that at the time, but now I do. I enjoy being in contact with the people on my beat and being there when they are in trouble and need help. The function of a supervisor is not to do the job of a cop, rather it is to assure that others are performing the street function. I am twenty-eight years old and have a lot of time to try to advance. Ultimately I would like to reach a rank that I will be able to attend the sixteen week FBI National Academy at Quantico, Virginia to learn police management and administration from working professionals."

Maleek sat at roll call and was assigned to the south end of District Four, which included the eastern side of the University of Cincinnati campus. The radio traffic was slow so he drove down to the one of the hospitals to write tickets for vehicles parked in bus stops. Vehicles parked in the stops created problems for the bus riders and other traffic because the bus would be unable to pull over to the curb.

Maleek was sitting in the cruiser writing his fourth ticket when the radio cracked, "9004, Officer needs assistance, shots fired Vine and Thill Street! 9004, I need a rescue unit, suspect has been shot." The 9000 series of numbers were assigned to the University Police Department on the City radio frequency. In a written memorandum of understanding between the City and the University, university cops were given the authority to patrol the streets around the campus and to enforce the traffic laws.

Maleek was only four blocks from the location and made a quick U-turn and screamed to the call for help. He was the second car to arrive at the scene and he saw an older model car crashed into a telephone pole. When he approached the car, he saw the African-American driver slumped in the driver's seat with blood dripping out of his left ear. It was clear to Maleek that the driver had expired. The campus cop that fired the shot was babbling incoherently that he felt he was in danger and had to shoot. Maleek looked at the cop, who looked to be about the same age as Maleek, and said, "Say nothing until you have an FOP lawyer with you. Are you injured? The campus cop answered, "Yes, I have some scrapes from falling into the street and pain in my back."

Police cars were now arriving in droves. A Sergeant arrived and Maleek told him, "A U.C. cop fired the shot and he is standing over there", pointing to a uniformed officer standing on the sidewalk. "The officer says he suffered scrapes from falling to the street. I think he needs to go to the hospital, boss." The Sergeant walked over to the officer and asked, "Do you need to go to the hospital Officer?" The officer nodded his head to indicate that he did.

The Sergeant told Maleek to take his cruiser and block the street at Vine Street and to allow no traffic to turn onto Thill. He also told Maleek, "If you are relieved of the traffic post, do not leave until the investigators get a chance to talk to you"

Maleek was told by the investigators to drive down to the Criminal Investigation Section in downtown Cincinnati so that they could get a written statement from him about what he saw when he first arrived. Maleek gave his statement and then returned to his beat.

***

Other than being the lead on all the news broadcasts, there was nothing that Maleek didn't know for the first week. Then he saw a television press conference where the Hamilton County Prosecutor excoriated the officer and called for the dissolution of the University of Cincinnati Police Department. The prosecutor told the media that he would be presenting the case to a Grand Jury seeking a Murder indictment against the officer. The Grand Jury came back with an indictment for Murder and the University summarily fired the officer.

***

As the trial date of the officer was quickly approaching, the Police Department was making plans for potential unrest. Personnel from all of the Districts were temporarily assigned to patrol the areas around the Courthouse, but were told to keep a low visibility. A contingent of bike patrol cops rode around the front of the Courthouse and moved everywhere the protestors went. They provided a buffer when the officer arrived for court until he got inside where he was met by uniformed deputy sheriffs who got him into the courtroom.

Throughout the two week trial Maleek and a few dozen other cops were within half a block of the Courthouse awaiting the outcome. They were told to bring riot gear in the event there were protests should a Not Guilty verdict result. Everyone was on high alert when the jury got the case and everyone was surprised that the case ended in a mistrial when the jury could not reach a verdict. There were protests demanding the prosecutor re-try the officer, but they were all peaceful. Maleek and the other officers were returned to their regular duty assignments.

CHAPTER SEVENTEEN

Maleek arrived at work and immediately saw the notice announcing an opening on the Special Weapons and Tactics Team. Large urban agencies like New York, Los Angeles, Dallas, Kansas City, Detroit and Columbus, Ohio have full time SWAT teams. When they are not out on a call, they are training. But cities like Cincinnati have as-needed Teams who have other full time assignments. Maleek grabbed the necessary form to apply and handed it to the supervisor. The team gets training days each month to hone their skills.

Two weeks later he was notified that he would be scheduled for phase one of the process, which would be the physical agility testing. The notification also stated that each phase would cause a reduction in the applicants and that there was only one current opening. Maleek cruised through the testing which including running with the almost one hundred pounds of equipment. He would move on to phase two.

Phase two was the shooting portion. Maleek's experience at FLETC gave him an advantage because he had to learn multiple weapons there. He passed that section as well and moved on to phase three.

Phase three involved tactical entry and, once again, Maleek had received specific training in that area at FLETC. He had already used flash bangs as a distraction device. The evaluators were impressed when Maleek threw a flash bang that penetrated the dry wall at the training house. He moved on to the final stage which was the interview.

The interviewers were the SWAT Commander, a Lieutenant, and two team leaders who were both Sergeants. The Lieutenant said, "This is a simple interview. We only want you to tell us why you want to join our team." Maleek paused for a moment and replied, "This is like my experience in football because it is a team effort. Everyone has a specific function and, when everyone performs their job, they will achieve success. The line protects the quarterback. The receivers run their routes and the quarterback throws the ball. If everyone performs, the play looks seamless, but if something goes awry then everyone else has to adapt. If the quarterback is under pressure, the receivers need to change their routes to get open. I would enjoy the structure of being a member of a team that is specifically trained to do a job."

Maleek got the single position and was issued the equipment necessary to do the job. He was assigned a marked police cruiser which would carry his equipment so that he would be able to respond to call-outs while running his beat. It was not a take home car, so he would have to drive to the District and pick up his cruiser should a call come when he was off-duty.

At the first training day Maleek was assigned to a five person team supervised by Sergeant Randy Rengling. Rengling's regular duty was at the Firearms Training Center attached to the Police Academy. He would be part of the breech team which makes the initial entry into the source of the problem.

***

Maleek was at home watching television with Mattie when his pager went off for a call out. He drove from home to the District and dressed to make the call. When he arrived at the staging area, Sergeant Rengling told the team that they would be serving a search warrant on a drug house and that the residence has two Dobermans who could present issues to the officers. There were believed to be armed suspects as well. Maleek would throw the flash bangs through the front window and two others would breach the front door with a battering ram. They were told that, if necessary, they were authorized to shoot the dogs. The team slowly approached the front door of the house and saw males in the family room. Maleek threw the flash bang through the window at the same time that the two officers at the front door yelled "POLICE, SEARCH WARRANT" and crashed the door open. The five officers made entry and heard the two dogs going wild in the back yard. One suspect tried to run toward the back door but Maleek intercepted him with a shoulder block and took him to the ground. Once the suspects had all been secured, the drug cops came in to search. The hit netted over one pound of heroin as well as scales to weigh the drugs and packaging materials. The suspects were taken away by uniforms and the team went back to the staging areas to secure their gear and go back to wherever they came from. The Sergeant was complimentary of all of the team when he de-briefed them.

Over the next six months Maleek had a total of nine callouts, all of which ended peacefully. Unlike what is seen on television, the Cincinnati Police SWAT team did not ever fire a single shot in its first thirty years of existence.

Maleek received a telephone call from the SWAT Commander Lieutenant Doug Venee to meet him at his office. When Maleek arrived, the Lt. asked, "Would you be interested in attending training to become a Hostage Negotiator?" Without hesitation, Maleek answered, "Of course I would."

Maleek was sent to the FBI Academy on the Quantico Marine Base in Quantico, Virginia for the week long training program. He listened intently as the mental health professionals and experienced negotiators told stories about their successes and their failures. They taught him de-escalation techniques that would help him to diffuse highly charged situations. Maleek returned to Cincinnati ready to get into his new role.

Maleek's first call as a negotiator was to an empty Christian church where an armed robbery suspect had run into. The suspect was behind the altar holding a gun to his own head. When Maleek arrived the team already had the perimeter of the church secured and had a sniper positioned on the second floor of the church. Maleek walked into the church and sat down in a pew in the first row. The suspect looked to be about twenty-one and had a semi-automatic handgun pointed to his head. Maleek looked up to the altar and said, "Hi, my name is Maleek, what's your first name? The young man said "Dave". Maleek said, "Okay Dave, I want this to come to a peaceful resolution, so how about we just talk?" The kid looked down and said, "I always wanted a job like your's." Maleek smiled and answered, "Flipping burgers is a job; law enforcement is a career." The suspect said, "You guys wouldn't shoot a person in a church" to which Maleek replied, "A church is just another building to us." They talked for about ten minutes and the young man laid the gun on the altar and walked to the front with his hands in the air. Maleek walked up

and escorted the suspect to the front door where he
was taken into custody without incident.

CHAPTER EIGHTEEN

Maleek was in roll call when he was handed a call for a burglary report on Paddock Hills Drive in the north end of the District. When the briefing was over Maleek got into the cruiser to answer the run. He was pissed because his coffee would have to wait until he completed the report. The resident of the house was a prominent Cincinnati businessman who reported losses in the area of one hundred thousand dollars in jewelry and electronics. Rather than use the radio to call for the crime scene techs, which would cause all the media trucks to show up, Maleek used the owner's home phone. He stayed at the scene until the techs arrived and then cleared the call.

Maleek picked up his coffee and pulled into the parking lot of Woodward High School to get caught up on his paperwork. It was just before eleven o'clock in the morning and the parking lot was filled with cars. Maleek had to park at the farthest end of the lot in the grass to be able to complete the report. He wanted it to be as complete as possible so that investigators would have all the available information. Maleek was concentrating on writing when the tones dropped on his police radio. "Attention all cars, all departments an all-county broadcast. Report of shots fired in the cafeteria, Woodward High School, 7000 Reading Road. Units available respond Code 3."

Maleek jumped out of the car and immediately activated his body worn camera, which would capture in detail the events that were about to happen. He ran full speed across the length of the school parking lot. When he arrived at the front door of the school, he screamed at the kids near the door asking where the cafeteria was located. The kids pointed in a direction. Malleek ran down the hallway yelling all the way. The kids all had their arms extended pointing him in the right direction. When he entered the cafeteria he saw the suspect running out an exterior door leading to the parking lot holding a semi-automatic handgun in his right hand, He saw kids laying on the floor. Some were bleeding and others were just scared. Maleek jumped over two bodies on the floor and gave chase. When he reached the exterior door the suspect had already made it half way through the parking and was moving in the direction of the football field. Maleek had his .40 caliber handgun out of the holster and used his other hand to update Police Communications of the status of the chase. Maleek was running full speed and was closing the distance between them. Maleek was yelling "STOP POLICE" every few steps, but the suspect had not even turned around to acknowledge that there was anyone behind him. The suspect jumped a small curb at the end of the lot and continued running into a grassy area with Maleek hot on his heels. Maleek saw the suspect raise the gun in his hand and begin to turn around and heard his ears ringing from the explosions of the two shots he fired. The suspect slowly crumpled to the ground falling face down onto the grass. Maleek slowly approached and kicked the gun away that the suspect had in his right hand. He used his foot to turn the suspect over onto his back and looked directly into the lifeless eyes and boyish face of the fourteen year old who had been holding a .380 semi-automatic pistol in his hand.

The boy's eyes looked directly into Maleek's soul and he was unable to break eye contact with the dead boy. The first backup officer arrived moments after the shots were fired. Dave Barnes had twenty-one years on the job and was a former runner-up in the Mister Cincinnati contest. Barnes would later tell officers that the look on Maleek's face actually scared him when he put his hand on the officer's shoulder and told him that everything was okay. Barnes softly asked Maleek to give him the gun and slowly gripped Maleek's right hand. Maleek had a death grip on the firearm with no intention of letting it be removed from his grip. Barnes pressed the release button causing the magazine to drop to the ground and then moved the slide back to eject a live cartridge in the chamber. Barnes then slowly pried each finger from the grip believing that he might well have to break fingers to get the weapon out of his hand. Maleek's eyes never left the dead young body on the ground.

Handing off Maleek's gun to another officer, Barnes spoke softly saying, "I need to get you out of here. We are here for you. Let me help you." Barnes softly, but forcefully, took control of his right arm, leading him away from the scene and toward the parking lot. Barnes walked him to the closest police car and yelled for the driver to come unlock it. A uniformed young female cop ran over and unlocked the doors and Barnes slowly placed Maleek in the back seat of the cruiser leaving the door opened. A Lieutenant who had just arrived ran up and ordered the female and Barnes to immediately take Maleek to University Hospital to get him checked out. He also ordered them to keep Maleek away from anyone other than medical personnel and make sure that he did not make any statements. The female officer asked Barnes whether or not to use the siren as she was afraid of startling Maleek, but Barnes said, "Drive like you have never driven lady, we need to get this cop to the hospital!" The medical staff at University Hospital

was waiting at the door when the police car arrived.
They placed Maleek on a stretcher and wheeled him
into the Emergency Room. A quick check showed no
physical injury and the resident ordered Maleek taken
upstairs to the Psych Unit. The two cops followed the
stretcher to the Fifth floor Psych Unit, stopping only to
secure their guns in a locker at the entrance.

CHAPTER NINETEEN

Dr. John Whitman had only recently completed his residency and was the only Psychiatrist on duty. He made a quick assessment of Maleek, who was still unresponsive to any verbal communication. The shrink told the two cops that it appeared that Maleek was experiencing traumatic shock and asked what happened that would have caused that. Barnes detailed the shooting and the Doc nodded his head. He ordered the nurse to administer a light sedative to help Maleek sleep and told the two cops that they were free to leave. Barnes stared the Doctor down saying, "We are under orders to stay with him. We aren't going anywhere."

***

Mattie was working in her vegetable garden in the back yard when she heard the front doorbell ring. She yelled, "I'm around back, come around." She watched the side yard as the large figure of the Police Chief and an Assistant Chief came into view with their white hats under their arms. A look of panic came on her face as she yelled, "Is my son okay?" The Chief motioned her to go inside and they entered the family room and sat down. The Chief said, "Maleek was involved in a shooting about an hour ago. He is physically fine, but was having problems mentally processing the incident. He is currently at University Hospital under the care of the doctors. I have a police car waiting outside to take you to see him."

When the marked cruiser pulled into the main entrance of the hospital, Mattie saw the media circus outside the door. There were live trucks, camera people and news reporters talking into microphones outside the door. The driver turned around and told Mattie, "When we get out, I want you to stay near me. We will protect you from the media rats. They will yell questions at you, but just ignore them and keep walking. Once we get into the hospital, you are safe."

The officer took her to the Psych Unit with Mattie watching intently as he checked his gun in the locker outside the entrance. Mattie saw at least twenty uniformed police officers of varying ranks standing around chatting. Her escort explained that they were there awaiting a report on the condition of her son. They were no sooner in the unit when a man in a white coat walked up to them. The man introduced himself saying, "Ms. Williams, I am Dr. Whitman, your son's physician. I ordered a light sedative to allow him to sleep, so he will not know that you are here." With that, the doctor led Mattie into the room where Maleek was peacefully sleeping. Mattie grabbed her son's hand and held it tightly. The doctor moved over to her and softly said, "We need to talk. Let's go to a conference room and I will try to explain to you what is happening with your son."

The two walked down to a room with Mattie's escort just a few steps behind. He waited outside the door as Mattie sat down in a chair. Dr. Whitman said, "Your son suffered what is known as traumatic shock from the incident. The brain goes into protective mode and shuts down when it reaches overload. We will not know about any damage until your son wakes up which should be twelve hours from now. The sleep allows the brain to settle down and relax, and we do not want to do anything which would alter that process. You should go home and come back in the morning. Know that we have the best staff in the region and your son will receive the highest quality of care."

The officer took Mattie home and asked if she needed anything before he left. When she told him she did not, he told her that he would pick her up at nine o'clock the next morning and stay with her for the day.

***

Mattie sat down in the family room after making her dinner and turned on the television. The first picture she saw on the news was of her surrounded by four large cops walking into the hospital. She watched as the Police Chief held a press conference where he refused to identify the officer involved in the shooting and would not give the frenzy of media zombies answers to their questions about what exactly happened. The Chief did tell them that four students had been shot and wounded by the suspect and that all were expected to survive. He also said that the officer had been transported to the hospital as a precautionary measure and that the police department was unsure when he would be available to be interviewed by investigators.

Mattie called Jamaal to make sure he knew that Maleek was physically okay and that she would hopefully be able to talk to him the next day. She was now exhausted from the stresses and went to bed.

***

When Maleek awoke at seven a.m., there was a nurse in his room. She immediately notified the senior attending psychiatrist, Dr. Frank Junz, who had been practicing for over thirty years. Dr. Junz entered the room moments later and sat down in a chair next to Maleek. He asked Maleek what he remembered of yesterday and was surprised by the officer's answer when. Maleek asked, "What happened yesterday and why am I here?" Dr. Junz thought for a moment and replied, "You were brought here by your fellow officers after an incident at Woodward High School. Do you remember being there?" Maleek thought for a moment and said, "All I remember s pulling into the parking lot to complete some reports and everything else is a blank. What happened next?" Dr. Junz said, "That is for a later time, I want your mind to have a chance to relax. I am going to give you some pills to decrease your anxiety and we will talk again. Your mother is on her way here to see you. She wants to make sure that you are okay."

Mattie arrived at the hospital to a different scene than the day before. There were no news trucks or groups of cops. Before she entered Dr. Junz stopped her and introduced himself. He cautioned her not to answer any of Maleek's questions about the incident and to keep the conversation light and airy. She went back to

Maleek's room and found him awake and alert. She hugged him and told him his brother wanted her to pass along his thoughts and prayers. Maleek immediately asked, "Do you know what happened that got me here, mom?" She looked at him and replied, "No, they haven't told me much yet. The Police Chief told me that he will update me as soon as they are sure what happened". It was clear that Maleek was going to push her for answers so she said, "I have to meet with your doctors this morning, so I only had a short time to stop and visit." With that, she left the room and Maleek was given another sedative to sleep as well as an anti-anxiety pill.

***

The Police Chief held a news conference at District One Headquarters. He told the media people that there was a surveillance video from the school which showed the events leading up to the officer involved shooting and that the officer's body camera also had captured the incident. He told them that the school video was being enhanced and that it would be released in the next couple of days after the Hamilton County Prosecutor had an opportunity to review it, but that, due to the age of the suspect, the body camera would not be released to the media.. He announced that the preliminary investigation seemed to show that the officer's actions were necessary and justified. The video was expected to substantiate that.

***

Dr. Junz walked into his office and picked up the phone. His call was to the psychologist who had devoted his working life to doing pre-employment screening and counselling for police officers. Dr. Don only knew what he had seen on television about the incident. After checking his records on the pre-employment testing, Dr. Don remembered Maleek as a calm, secure, athletic and highly competitive young man. If anyone could overcome the traumatic shock of this incident, it would be this kid.

Dr. Junz wanted Dr. Don to collaborate in the treatment plan for Maleek, and Dr. Don said he would be glad to offer any possible assistance.

CHAPTER TWENTY

The Police Chief called another press conference to release the surveillance video from the school. The room at District One was filled with local and national media eagerly wanting answers to the killing of a fourteen year old boy. The Chief began the briefing by telling everyone that they would see the video untouched, then see an enhanced version of the video. The reason for showing both versions was that no one could then claim that the editing has changed the actual event as it occurred. The Chief continued to refuse to release the body camera footage out of deference to the family .because it showed the child up close. He told the media they would have to sue to have it released, but that the family had been shown the unedited video in its entirety

The first run of the video captured by the school was from a long distance away from the actual scene. It showed the suspect running in the grass with the officer close behind. The same video was shown with a zoomed in shot of the young boy with a gun in his right hand. A closer zoom showed the boy lifting the weapon and beginning to turn to his left when the officer fired twice. The Chief told the media that one shot entered the upper left side of the boy's back and the other shot entered the body just below the left armpit entering the heart and causing death.

The Hamilton County Prosecutor then stood up and told the media that his office and the parents of the young boy watched the video in its original form and then watched the enhanced versions. The Prosecutor said it was his decision that there would be no criminal charges against the officer, and that the whole incident was tragic for all. The parents had also been shown the officer's body cam footage.

***

Maleek was brought into a treatment that looked more like a family room with soft colors and comfortable seats. His two doctors chatted with Maleek about his high school and college football experiences, when Doctor Don suddenly asked, "Maleek, what is it that you see in your dreams?" Maleek's facial expression suddenly changed and he answered in a soft voice, "I see the face of a boy with lifeless eyes staring up at me and that scares me to death."

Dr. Junz motioned for an attendant to come into the room and told him to take Maleek down to the Physical Therapy area and show him the equipment so Maleek could work out. As the two were leaving, Dr. Junz told the attendant, "I want you to watch his mood and facial expressions and report back to me."

When Maleek walked into the PT room, his face lit up when he saw the treadmill in the middle of the room. He set the grade at twenty percent and kicked the speed up to running and was almost immediately in the "zone." The attendant watched intently as the miles display continued to run up. Maleek was still running strong at the fifteen mile marker and looked like he could go for hours. When he finally stepped off

the machine, he went to the weights and loaded three
hundred pounds, doing bench presses, pull ups and
squats. He was covered with sweat when he called it
a day asking, "Where can I go to get a shower?" The
attendant smiled and told him that he could get his
shower back at the unit. After taking a long shower,
Maleek was given another light sedative and slept the
full night.

***

Russell Damon Woosnam was the oldest of three
children in a loving family. His parents both worked in
order to be able to provide their children a Catholic
elementary education. But when it came time for
Woosey, his nickname of his parents, it did not matter
how they crunched the numbers that they could pay
the tuition for a Catholic high school. They researched
every school in the Cincinnati Public School system in
an attempt to find something that would Woosey
might find challenging and enjoyable. Beginning at
age ten, Woosey would go into his room while the
other two youngsters went outside to play with the
other neighborhood children, and write the code
necessary to make his animated figures accept the
commands from a joystick for the video game he was
creating.

Woodward High School is in the north end of
Cincinnati and would be a forty minute bus ride each
way, but it offered a high technology track that would
suit the creative side of the oldest boy. In his first
week at the new school, Woosey experienced things
that he never knew in the Catholic school system. The
students were mean, unruly, and had no respect for
any authority. They controlled the classroom and the

teachers were powerless. Fights were a common occurrence and the adults actually seemed afraid. Woosey walked into the boy's restroom and was almost immediately pinned to a wall by a bully who demanded his lunch money. After that incident, Woosey would not use the restroom during school hours. In the cafeteria, he would be the butt of jokes from many students and was not able to make any friends at the school. His frustration and anger changed him from a reserved and polite young boy into a depressed and angry young man.

It was a Saturday morning when Woosey went to the breakfast table and his parents told him they had all been invited to his uncle's house for a cook out. While the rest of the children played in the yard, Woosey went into his uncle's office to work on his game on the computer. After completing some tasks, Woosey found that he had not brought a thumb drive to store his work so he opened the desk drawers to find one. Under a cloth in a drawer was his uncle's .380 semi-automatic pistol. The small gun fit perfectly in his pocket and he replaced the cloth that was covering it. When he left for school on Monday morning, he put the gun into his right pocket and ran to catch the bus. At lunch time, he walked into the cafeteria and directly toward the bully who stole his money and the bully's girlfriend who had berated him. He pulled the gun out and fired four shots. The first hit the bully in the left shoulder, the second in the right arm of the girlfriend. The third and fourth missed their intended target, one hitting a boy in the leg and the other grazing the stomach of a girl who was just walking by. Woosey then ran out of the back entrance and into the parking lot of the school. He heard the deep voice of a male behind him yelling, "STOP, POLICE", but he kept on running. When he reached the end of the lot, he jumped a curb and ran into a grass field that led to the football stadium. Woosey could hear the footsteps gaining ground on him and knew how deeply disappointed his parents would be of what he had done. He made a decision at that moment that this needed to end. He raised the arm with the gun and started to turn when the two bullets entered his body. The first exploded his heart and the second perforated his lung. He fell forward onto his knees and then face-down into the grass. When the cop rolled him over, his eyes looked up at the cop asking, "Mister, why did you have to kill me?"

***

The two doctors met to discuss Maleek's treatment while he was down in the gym working out. Dr. Junz said, "The hospital, over my strenuous objection, has ordered me to release Maleek tomorrow morning. I think you should take the lead on the treatment and I will prescribe whatever medications he needs." Dr. Don agreed and said, "I am thinking three sessions a week and the Cincinnati Police Peer support group once a week."

CHAPTER TWENTY-ONE

There was a cruiser waiting to take him home when Maleek was released from the hospital in the morning. The Commander of District Four had already ordered two cops to put Maleek's car in his driveway and they had given the keys to Mattie.

Maleek was given pills for depression, pills to help him sleep and pills to help him function while awake. On the recommendation of Dr. Don, Maleek's badge was returned to him, but his gunbelt and firearm were kept by the department. Dr. Don wrote in a report to the Police Chief that, "Returning the officer's weapon at this time could be detrimental because of his extremely fragile mental state."

Cincinnati has a status called "Injured with Pay" by which officer(s) receive their regular pay if they are injured in the line of duty. The City terminated Maleek's IWP status as soon as he was released from the hospital and he was forced to start using his accrued sick leave. As he had not used a single sick day in his time on the department, he had the maximum amount of days allowed.

The stream of people coming to the house to make sure he was doing well was continuous and everyone passed along good wishes and offered any assistance he needed. Maleek started his three meetings a week with Dr. Don and attended his first Peer Support Group meeting. The Peer Support Group is made up of officers who have been involved in police shootings or in-custody deaths. They help each other get through the traumatic experience. Some of the officers have decades of experience and others with little experience. Cincinnati Police do not have a lot of uses of deadly force when compared to other urban police departments, but wanted any officer to have an outlet to express their experience and feelings.

The one hour sessions with Dr. Don were not bearing a lot of fruit in the first two months. Dr. Don would ask Maleek to talk about his feelings since the last meeting, but the two never discussed the details of the event. As far as the Peer Group, Maleek did nothing but sit and listen to other officers and, after five weeks, gave up attending.

It had now been three months since the event and Dr. Don asked Maleek, "What do you remember about the incident?" Maleek replied, "I was sitting in the cruiser writing a report when the call came out over the radio. I remember running across the parking lot and entering the front door. I remember entering the cafeteria and seeing the suspect running out the back door. I chased him across the parking lot and he turned toward me and was raising the gun in his hand. I remember hearing the shots ring out and seeing him crumple to the ground. When I turned him over, I saw it was just a kid." Don softly asked, "Maleek, when do you think you knew how young the suspect was?" Maleek answered, "I didn't until I turned him over." Dr. Don said, "That is the point. You did not know it was a child and you simply reacted to his actions which placed you in jeopardy. You did what your training taught you." Maleek thought for a moment and said, "The boy's eyes burned a hole into my soul. That hole opens up every time I close my eyes."

Maleek's sick time pay was running out and there was not enough evidence of improvement to declare him 'fit for duty.' The FOP sent out a plea to its members to donate their sick time to Maleek so that he could make a full recovery and return to duty. The FOP was able to get him an additional one hundred and twenty days.

***

Maleek had completed a session when Dr. Don said, I have something I want you to do on your way home. I want you to drive by the District today. You do not have to stop, but we need to see if there will be any reaction to see your workplace." Maleek went out of his way to pass the Police Station and reported to Dr. Don that there were no adverse reactions. At the next session Dr. Don told him, "Today I want you to pull your car into the District parking lot. If you feel up to it, walk inside and say hello to the officers there. If you don't feel up to it, just leave and drive on home. We want to test your limits. If you have any problems, call me immediately."

Maleek drove into the lot where the cops park for their shift and turned off the ignition of the Cadillac. He sat for a short time and suddenly began shaking uncontrollably. He quickly started his car and left the lot and drove home. He forgot to call the Doctor.

When he told Dr. Don what occurred at his next session Dr. Don said, "I ask my patients for total honesty and I owe them the same treatment. Regrettably, your law enforcement career is over. I will be submitting a report to the City recommending that they give you a medical disability. I am with you today and I will be available to you for as long as you feel you need me. You will reach a point where you

can utilize your education and experience and live a
very productive life. This was never your fault and you
did everything by the numbers. But human response
is not something over which we have no control.

CHAPTER TWENTY-TWO

In the first three weeks that Maleek had been home there was a steady line of well-wishers stopping by to see if they could offer him any assistance. Officers from the FOP and the Sentinels as well as cops he had worked with in the different districts and the SWAT team members offered to take him to University of Cincinnati and Xavier basketball games, Cyclone hockey and to the FOP Lodge to relax. Mattie asked him to take her to a Roger Bacon football game and David Vesper offered to run with him or take him to the Boys and Girls club.

Maleek received calls from the Cincinnati Bengals and the Carolina Panthers pro football teams inviting him to practice with them.

Whether caused by the prescription drugs he was taken or just pure depression, Maleek showed no interest in any of the offers that were made. He would spend all of his alone time laying on his bed watching old time television shows like *Gunsmoke, Get Smart, Father Knows Best and Bewitched.* When he came out for dinner, he would tell Mattie to turn off the local and national news because he did not want to watch it.

***

Mattie walked into Maleek's room and handed him an envelope from the Ohio Police Pension Board. Maleek opened the letter which said, "We have reviewed all of the documentation submitted in your claim for benefits and have determined that you will be required to be evaluated by one of our staff physicians. Please schedule an appointment within the next thirty days at the State Office Building in Columbus, Ohio. A determination will be issued after that evaluation." Maleek took the letter to Dr. Don, who told Maleek that he would personally drive Maleek to the appointment.

The two arrived at the State Building and Dr. Don told Maleek to sit in the waiting room while he met with the State shrink. Maleek sat quietly for about thirty minutes and then saw Dr. Don coming out of the back. Dr. Don motioned to Maleek and said, "The doctor is ready to see you now." Maleek was escorted back to a treatment room where an older white doctor was seated at a desk. The man rose from his chair and extended his hand out and said, "My name is Dr. Stephen Keenen and I work for the State of Ohio. It is really nice to meet you, Maleek. Have a seat and let's just chat."

Maleek shook the doctor's hand and was mildly surprised at the strength of the man's grip. He sat in a chair and the doctor said, "I have just had a long chat with Dr. Don and I only have a couple of questions for you. Can you tell me, in your own words, about the incident itself?"

Maleek methodically walked through the school incident from its inception without any visible emotion, but when he reached the actual shooting, the doctor noticed that Maleek's voice began cracking, his hands were visibly trembling and his eyes were welling up with tears. When Maleek was done talking the doctor asked, "What happened in the parking lot of the police station?" Maleek paused for a moment and answered, "I was following the directions of Dr. Don to pull into the police parking lot. I parked my car and turned off the engine intending to walk into the District as I was feeling pretty good. I reached for the door latch and experienced a sense of terror. I started shaking uncontrollably and felt an immediate need to escape. Dr. Don told me to call him if there were any problems, but I could not even dial my phone because I was shaking so bad. I started the car and quickly drove out of the lot and then home." Dr. Keenen said, "I thank you for your candor and honesty and you are under good care with Dr. Don. You will receive the Board's determination within the next thirty days. I wish you the best of luck."

Maleek told Dr. Don about the session on the hour and one half drive back to Cincinnati. Dr. Don told him not to worry, that his claim would be allowed.

Two weeks later Mattie came into the bedroom and handed him a certified letter from the Pension Board. The letter said, "The Board has reviewed all of the appropriate documentation and the report of our Physician. It is our determination that your request for Medical Disability is hereby granted and you will receive compensation back to the date of the application. You are also eligible for health insurance through us at a cost of six hundred and fifty dollars per month for the individual policy. This determination does not preclude you from seeking employment in any field with the exclusion of law enforcement and there are no limitations on the income you are authorized to earn.

CHAPTER TWENTY- THREE

Mattie was watching Maleek's mental state deteriorate on a daily basis. She finally reached a point where she called David Vesper to get his help. Vesper listened carefully to what Mattie had to say and said, "Give me the day. I will be over tomorrow to see him and hopefully I will have some kind of help to offer.

Mattie walked into Maleek's room the next day and saw he was watching television. She told him, "David Vesper is here and said he needs to talk to you." Maleek turned off the episode of _Gunsmoke_ he was watching and walked into the family room where Vesper was sitting on the couch. Vesper said, "We need to go for a ride. I need to talk with you." The two went out to Vesper's car and as soon as they got in Vesper said, "Here is the deal. Your police pension is not going to provide a liveable income for you and your mother and you have never paid into Social Security to get any money from them. You need to find something to generate money and I have a business opportunity for you to consider."

Vesper took Maleek to a warehouse and showed him a sand blasting business that Maleek and his brother could start. Vesper said, "The work will be hard, but that is what you need to take your mind off the events of the past. I made some calls and got you a small business loan of seventy-five thousand dollars for the startup money you will need and called a Bengals fan who happens to own a trash collection company. He is willing give you a contract to strip the paint off of their trucks so that they can re-paint them. You will need to buy a truck to carry the pot that holds the coal slag needed to do the blasting and an air compressor to operate it."

The sales representative told Maleek that he would receive training in the use of the equipment and that the training would take less than two days.

Maleek called Jameel and told him about the opportunity and Jameel sounded excited at the possibilities of building a business. Maleek and Jameel went out and purchased a Ford F350 dual wheel truck and then purchased a used air compressor. Jameel said the equipment could be stored at his auto shop and he would cease the operation of that business.

***

Maleek was methodical in removing all of the lights on the large garbage truck placing them in the driver's seat so that the company would be able to find them. He covered the cab of the truck with a large tarp so that the windows would not be damaged by the spray. He had to don a safety suit with a hose to provide him oxygen because of the spray of the slag. He stripped the paint of the truck inch by inch assuring that the painters would not have any issues when their turn came. Jameel sat in the company truck outside of the enclosed blasting area to assure that the compressor did not malfunction which would cut off the oxygen that Maleek needed to breathe. It took just less than seven hours to complete the job and Maleek told Jameel that it was the best seven hours he had in months.

With each passing day Maleek became excited to leave the house in the morning to go to work. Another cop got him a contract with a municipal township to blast and paint five hundred fire hydrants per year. The FOP got him a minority contract to remove graffiti from City property and he received leads to help strip antique cars that people were restoring.

After six month of operation, the business was beginning to flourish. Every minute that Maleek could focus on his task was a minute that he was not thinking about the stare of a dead fourteen year old boy that he had killed asking, "Mister, why did you kill me?" He was actually beginning to sleep without the assistance of drugs.

***

Two years into the business, Maleek needed to hire people to help him with the fire hydrant portion of the business because it required painting the hydrants after they were blasted and flaggers to control the flow of traffic when they had to block a lane of traffic on busy roadways. He was able to find a few retired cops who were just looking for something to keep themselves busy and things were running well.

***

Maleek rarely took the after-hours calls for the business, but Jamaal had a dance recital with his daughter. This call was from Police Communications because the brothers had a contract with the City of Cincinnati to remove gang graffiti and they were needed at Lynn and Baymiller in the City's West End. Maleek drove to the storage area and got in the company truck to remove the unwanted paint. When he arrived there were two cruisers parked nearby to provide him security while he worked. As soon as he saw the uniformed cops, a sense of panic overtook him. He tried not to make eye contact with the two cops who were trying to be friendly and engage him in a bit of conversation. Maleek focused his total attention on cleaning every inch of the wall bearing the gang signs that he recognized from his days on the street. When he was done with his work, Maleek walked over to the two cops and said, "I need to apologize to you, I really am not a prick. I used to be a Cincinnati cop until I was involved in a shooting four years ago. I have had issues with seeing cops ever since." The one cop, who was also African-American, looked at Maleek and said, "No problem man, now I know why you look familiar."

Maleek drove back to the shop and tears rolled down his face.

CHAPTER TWENTY-FOUR

Mattie was sleeping when her phone rang at six o'clock in the morning. She was groggy when she answered only to hear the voice of Jameel who said, "Mother, Maleek didn't come to work this morning and we have a job in a half an hour. I tried to call him but only got his voice mail. Can you check and see if maybe he overslept?"

Mattie put on a robe and walked into Maleek's bedroom and saw he was laying on his back. She called out his name several times and then walked over to the bed and shook him. His skin was almost cold and he was not responding to her. She felt his neck and could not feel a pulse. She panicked and told Jameel, "I need to call 9-1-1, I think he might be dead."

It took only minutes for the paramedics to arrive. They checked him out and the senior medic told Mattie, "I am sorry, but he has been dead for several hours. I need to call a police supervisor to come out because it is our policy."

Sergeant Darnell Brand arrived at the house thirty minutes later. He told Mattie that, "Maleek worked under me when he was assigned to District Five so I want to walk you through what will happen. I will call for a Coroner's van to come remove him and he will be taken to the Coroner's Office for an autopsy because of his age and the fact that he has no known ailments."

Shortly after the request was made, the Coroner's van arrived at the house with a deputy sheriff driving and two prisoners from the jail to remove the body. Brand told Mattie that, "They will put Maleek into a black body bag to transport him to the morgue. You might not want to watch this process." Mattie looked defiantly at the cop and said, "I will be totally involved with every step in the process because this is my son. I understand that I will not be allowed to ride with him or be at the autopsy, but I want to know everything about what happened to him."

***

At the autopsy the pathologist reported a physically fit thirty-four year old male with no visible sign of injury or disease. He sent blood and tissue samples to the crime lab for toxicology testing and declared the death being by natural causes pending the toxicology results. When the results came back negative, the death certificate listed "Undetermined natural causes."

***

Mattie received a call from the President of the Fraternal Order of Police the day after Maleek's passing. He told Mattie that the City declined to declare Maleek's death as a line of duty death, so they would not be helping with the planning or expenses associated with a funeral service. The FOP would pick up the expenses for any service, but officers who want to attend would have to do so on their own time or take the time off. There would be no honor guard or escorts unless it was done by people who get to take home their marked police cruiser. He told her that the FOP would be in contact the next day. When he hung up Mattie began crying uncontrollably.

The FOP planned the service at the same Catholic Church in downtown Cincinnati that on-duty deaths had been held. The Honor Guard had all put in for personal time off work to attend and pay tribute to Maleek for his service. Canine cops would provide an escort for the funeral procession and the Cincinnati Police chaplain would officiate. The Cincinnati Fire Department union also wanted to participate to the level that they were allowed and firefighters who were not on-duty would be present in their uniforms. Members of the SWAT team would be the pallbearers for the service.

There were about two hundred who attended the service at St. Peter in Chains cathedral. David Vesper spoke to meeting an eighth grade student and watching him mature into a great police officer. Because it was not a line of duty death, there were no politicians or the Police Chief espousing the great things that Maleek was able to accomplish.

Mattie was the last speaker. She had to be helped up the steps to the altar and her voice was cracking as she said, "I want to apologize because I am not an educated woman. I was told to write down what I wanted to say, but decided that I would rather be honest. My son did great things with his life and I will celebrate that until the day that I die. He put his best effort into everything that he did. When offered scholarships to the best football programs in the country, he only asked one question. What kind of Criminal Justice program does your school offer? Had he chosen a different school, there is a likelihood that he would have been drafted by a professional team, but that was not the path that he chose. All he wanted to do was be a policeman. He wanted to serve the people of Cincinnati and he did it honorably. The autopsy says that his death was Undetermined Natural Causes, but the fact is that I know what killed my son. Maleek Williams died of a broken heart. It is that simple. He was never able to recover from taking the life of a fourteen year old boy whose cold dead eyes looked into Maleek's soul and asked, 'Mister, why did you have to kill me!' No police officer should ever have to experience a situation of that magnitude. I leave you with this. Serve the citizens of Cincinnati, Ohio with the energy and compassion of my son. Be safe in your travels and know that I love all of you.